Bluebeard's Castle

Bluebeard's Castle

GENE KEMP

faber and faber

First published in 2000
by Faber and Faber Limited
3 Queen Square London WCIN 3AU
Published in the United States by Faber and Faber Inc.,
an affiliate of Farrar, Straus and Giroux, New York

Photoset by RefineCatch, Broad Street, Bungay, Suffolk
Printed in England by Mackays of Chatham plc, Chatham, Kent

A CIP record for this book
is available from the British Library

ISBN 0–571–19318–8

2 4 6 8 10 9 7 5 3 1

To all those people who didn't like the book.

As soon as they returned home the marriage was con-
cluded. About a month afterwards the Blue Beard told
his wife that he was obliged to take a journey into a
distant country for six weeks at least, about an affair of
very great consequence, desiring her to divert herself in
his absence, send for her friends and acquaintances,
carry them into the country, if she pleased, and make
good cheer wherever she was: Here, said he, are the
keys of the two great rooms that hold my best and richest furniture; these are of my silver and gold plate,
which is not to be made use of every day; these open
my strong boxes, which hold my gold and silver money;
these my caskets of jewels; and this is the master-key
that opens all my apartments: But for this little one
here, it is the key of the closet at the end of the great
gallery on the ground floor. Open them all, go into all
and every one except that little closet, which I forbid
you, and forbid you in such a manner, that if you happen to open it, there is nothing but what you may
expect from my just anger and resentment. She promised to observe every thing he order'd her, who, after
having embraced her, got into his coach and proceeded
on his journey.

Charles Perrault, 'The Story of Bluebeard'

Part One

One

It all began that summer holiday when a television crew came to our street filming a story about life in Victorian England, but not the posh sort with bonnets and crinolines, the rough sort with ragged clothes and horse-mucky streets.

My mother didn't think much of this.

'Not Victorian Times again!' she cried. 'I don't want them *here*! Our street's special, wonderful. Lovely little houses all painted different. Don't want us looking like garbage on telly!'

She knows about the street, Mum does. Everybody ends up on our doorstep with problems, spare friends and relatives and chat. 'Hang up your Hang-Ups Here!' is her motto.

But that day everybody was over the moon.

The telly crowd filled up the street, stopping the traffic at one end; it's a little street with a cul-de-sac at the other end so you can't drive through. There were people on rooftops, people on car-tops, people lying flat on pavements and drains, cameras everywhere, dozens of smoke machines and a bloke walking round holding an upside-down sweeping brush. He was very friendly and talked to my mate Slug and me, and we found out that it wasn't an upside-down sweeping brush but an important piece of equipment and that there was to be a church burned down, the corner shop robbed and a riot at the pub, so lots of fun and walk-on parts for everybody. And Dressing Up! We were high as kites. We'd be on telly. We'd be FAMOUS. Everyone (except my mother) wanted their face on the screen. It was all luvvy-duvvy and when it was finished there'd be a street party with cakes and champagne, crisps and sweets and Coke – no, it's OK, Mum, not *that* sort, I said, as Mum moaned and rabbited on.

'You wanna bet?' she snapped back. 'It'll be everywhere.'

Every day the street was crowded. Famous faces came and went. We sat on our doorstep watching them come and go, naming names and guessing.

'Not much glamour in real life, have they?' said my sister Marie. 'Dead ugly, some of 'em.'

Very soon someone spotted her. People always do. She's got eyes like saucers and hair like a volcano exploding.

'Hey, we'd like the pretty one. You there, you, with the afflicted looking kid in the buggy. Yes, you.'

'That's my sister Ems in the buggy. And she's not afflicted. She's bright,' snapped Marie.

'She just looks that way,' I put in. 'Like E.T.'

'Well, we'll have you and Ems. And you two . . .' This was my friend Slug and me. 'You can be dirty, rascally street urchins. You won't have to do anything. Just be yourselves.'

So we all stood around – waited – stood around – waited – acted a tiny bit – stood around – waited. Take one – take two – take three – take four – take ninety-nine, take one – take on and on. And on.

'Brilliant,' they said about Marie. 'Such talent. A natural.'

'I know,' said Marie.

'All this will do no good at all,' my mother muttered. 'It'll end in tears. You'll see.'

Day after day they cleaned the street up. Next day everything was altered, then dirtied down again. Everything was pulled to bits and put back again.

Neighbours fell out.

Families stopped speaking to each other.

The weather turned thundery.

Tempers got horrible and grew worse.

Those without parts hated those with parts.

Everyone wanted a bigger part.

Everyone bossed everyone else.

Everybody hated everybody else.

'The grown-ups are worse than the kids,' said Marie.

'They always are,' my mother sighed.

In the middle of it all, sitting on his Director's chair, was a small man with grey curls, bright eyes and blue designer stubble on his chin. Round him hovered big, bald men with earrings, little ratty men and women with clever faces, large earrings and big teeth. The men didn't speak. The women never stopped. All this went on and on through the endless hot August. Me and Slug, Marie and Ems watched and acted, acted and watched.

'Our street will never be the same again,' my mother groaned. 'It's changed for ever.'

So was our family.

All this time our big sister Sharon was up north with her boyfriend Marshy, either tunnelling underground or tying themselves to trees.

Marshy and Sharon are road protesters and they're into Saving the Planet. So she wasn't here while this film was being made. In fact, I think they were probably being filmed up north. Marshy is quite famous up there.

We've known him for yonks as he lived in the street, but then he began to get known for protests and trees and tunnels and Sharon went after him, dumping her GCSEs and us as well. Not that *we* cared, as she always treated us like dung-beetles, but it upset Mum, who'd hoped she'd stick to her studies. No way, laughed Sharon, disappearing through the door.

Now Marie and Ems, Slug and me were on our steps in the crowded street when Sharon turned up with a face like a bad August thunderstorm. Just like the weather in the street, in fact. The film was nearly finished and everyone was frantic, crazy, barmy, and it was boiling hot.

'What's all this, then? Git outta my way,' Sharon bellowed and kicked her booted feet at what turned out to be the chief cameraman so that he fell down the steps, breaking his ankle and shouting a lot.

The cameraman was lifted up and Sharon was seized. Just like that.

They dragged her over to Blue Stubble on his

Director's chair. Marie, Slug, Ems and me struggled behind through the crowd, now gone quiet. We could hear the groans of the cameraman.

A First Aid team was dealing with him. Sharon was pushed forward.

'SAVE THE PLANET!' she cried.

'Where's Marshy?' Slug asked me. 'Can't see him anywhere.'

Marshy had vamoosed. He's like that. Twin to the Invisible Man. (Sharon's noisy, though, has a lot to say.)

Blue Stubble stared at Sharon long enough for me to see a razor-sharp, foxy face behind the nice cosy fuzzy look and the sparkly eyes.

He scared me. Marie clutched me. I knew she was ready to leap forward – she's like that – to defend Sharon, who's horrible, but she is our sister and we gotter stand wiv'er!

There Sharon stood in front of Blue Stubble, with her woolly plaited head, her tattoos, her eight earrings on one ear, her nose-ring, her dirty rags and tags.

She had stopped shouting.

Nobody spoke except Marie, pushing forward as near as she could, crying, 'Let her go! Let her go!'

People held Sharon's arms. At least she couldn't punch the bloke, I hoped. She does sometimes, if she feels that way.

'Why you cluttering our place up with this muck?' she spat out, instead.

Blue Stubble just sat looking. Then . . . 'Want a part in my film?' he asked, gently.

'Get lost,' she answered, and this time spat out her chewing gum on to one of his blue suede desert boots. 'I wun't be seen dead in *your* snotty little film. I gotta life in the real world.'

Silence, then a great noise like a lorry emptying a load of gravel. She'd said 'No!' She'd said NO to the Director. She'd said NO to being on telly. Surprise, surprise. Except us. We *know* what Sharon's like. She can say no to anything or anyone, but it's usually us and Mum.

This guy just stared at her from her woolly head to her muddy boots. Then he clicked his fingers. Four people stepped forward.

'She's filthy. Clean her up. Then take her back to my place. I want to take a good look at her.'

Sharon spat on the other boot.

'No,' screamed Marie. 'No, no. Don't let them, Sharon! Help! Don't let them take her away, everybody,' she appealed, sobbing. No one moved except Slug, who tried to get to them.

Marie made a grab at Sharon, but was pushed aside.

'Sharon, don't go!' Marie screamed. 'Gary, David (Slug's real name), help me! Don't let them take her away. Get Mum. Sharon's being kidnapped. Get our mum, somebody. She'll stop them.'

'Who are those kids?' asked Blue Stubble.

'My family. Wanna make summat of it?' Sharon snapped.

Marie turned to the crowd, crying, 'Help! Help! Get my mum.'

'Good acting, innit?' somebody said.

But Mum was busy trying to get an ambulance for Mrs Birkinshaw next door who was suffering from asthma. My mum's her nurse. The ambulance couldn't get into the street. But the car carrying off Sharon got away easily.

And we were left standing in the crowd while Marie wept, Ems licked a lolly someone had given her and the cameraman was transported to the Out-Patients, still swearing about his ankle.

Then the storm broke. Lightning, thunder, rain, hail, blackness. In two minutes the street was empty.

Two

There was no street party.

'I didn't think there would be,' my mother said.

No Sharon came home.

'She'll be down a hole with Marshy,' I said. 'Or up a tree.'

'Dunno,' said Marie.

'Where is Marshy?' asked Slug.

'Dunno,' said Marie.

But she stuck some bits from the newspaper in her school jotter.

MILLIONAIRE GIVES UP ON MAKING MOVIES

No more films from the master film maker Magnus Moore for the moment. 'I've got new interests in life,' he told our reporter Polly Sims in an exclusive interview in his eight-million-pounds Kensington mansion. He had just flown in from New York. 'I've got a whole, fresh, exciting project to develop over here,' he told her.

Magnus Moore, the well-known movie king, is planning to develop his theme park to become the biggest ever to be seen in our Lovely Heritage Island. His famous Moore Castle is situated miles from anywhere, surrounded by a moat and thousands of trees in the Moore Grave Forest. As well as the Moore Theme Park there will be prize collections of animals, cars, circuses, stamps, butterflies. You name it, Magnus will have Moore of it, Ha! Ha!

Our reporter Polly Sims is on the spot, keeping you informed.

Magnus Moore is 49.

She'd cut out a small paragraph from the bottom the last page:

Nothing more has been heard of Polly Sims, our reporter missing in the Moore Grave Forest for two weeks now. She had been reporting on the new Moore Happiness Theme Park now being built there.

Magnus Moore is 59.

I was jolly pleased Marie was busy with her

scrapbooks because you never know what it's going to be with her.

'I want adventures,' she cries, 'I must have adventures. I can't live without adventures. Magic, mystery, flying to the moon! That's for me, me, ME-EE-EE.'

It could be anything – getting a thorn out of a lion's paw, for instance. She's always going on about a Roman geezer who did just that and then the lion saved him in the Colosseum later. Fat chance in my case. With my luck I'd help the most ungrateful lion in captivity and get gobbled up in a second. Once she made me climb on the roof to rescue a kitten stuck there. The kitten scratched me, then hopped down easily while the fire brigade had to rescue me instead. They rabbited on for ages. So did my mum. This sort of thing happens over and over again. *And I always get into trouble. Not her. Not fair.*

My mum was spending all her spare time at the police station trying to trace Sharon. Trouble was, they didn't think for one minute she'd been kidnapped. They thought she'd gone off on a runaround. Mum tried to get hold of Dad, but he was on a sponsored walk for oil-rig orphans.

Three

I could hear Ems shrieking the place down. Slug leapt up to rescue her and I followed slowly. Mum had already rushed down the stairs into the hall and picked her up.

'There, there,' she soothed. 'It's only your father.'

A big, tough, hairy man stood in the hall. He reached out for Ems and tried to kiss her. She bit him.

'Ouch,' he cried, holding his cheek. 'What a welcome!'

'It's only because she hasn't seen you for ages,' explained Mum, pecking his other cheek. 'She's been told not to go with strange men.'

'But I'm not a strange man. I'm her father.'

I felt sorry for him. So I went forward and shook him by the hand, which took him by surprise as well as me. I liked him. It felt great to have another man in the family with people like my mother, Sharon, Ems and Marie about. I mean, I know Slug's always here and he's a boy, but it's not the same, is it? You don't think of Slug as anything.

Then Marie came in, leapt on him and started all that kissing rubbish and asking if he'd brought us presents and how long was he here for and could he stay with us all the time now, please? She told Ems to be good and smile at her dad and Ems thought about it and managed half one and let him pick her up and she tugged his beard hard, then pinched his nose and pulled his ears.

When he'd stopped squeaking he asked Mum, 'Well, what's it all about, then? I couldn't follow you on the phone and half your letter was missing.'

'Oh, yes. I was in the middle of a letter to you, telling you all about it when Mrs Birkinshaw fell down the stairs – she's really accident prone, that woman – so I had to go and help her, and when I got back Ems had got hold of that letter, licked it, and thrown half of it away down the street, but it still got posted.'

'Well, let's hear what it's all about, then. Come on, Nellie.'

My dad's on an oil rig in the North Sea and doesn't get home much. Mum says you can date the times he comes home from us – Sharon,

Marie, me and Ems, the apple of her eye. He and Mum get on famously, she says, as long as they don't meet too often. He's got his work (drilling oil) and she's got hers (looking after Mrs Birkinshaw). And us.

'Where's the prezzies?' we all yelled, crowding down the hall and into the kitchen.

Slug was looking miserable as he's not really part of the family so he didn't think he'd get one. He's always *with* us because he lives next door and he's a lonely only 'un. Sharon says his mum and dad took one look at him when he was born and didn't want to know. So he's left on his own a lot. Marie's kind to him and he thinks she's a wonder, which she is, I suppose. I just wish she'd leave me alone.

But Dad had got something for him as well, so that was OK. Then he looked round.

'Right, tell me the worst. What's Sharon up to?'

'She's been kidnapped. Oh, Jack, what shall we do?'

'Do? I'll tell you what I shan't do. I'm not paying any ransom money! Not for Sharon! Besides, I haven't got any.'

At that moment the hall door flew open again, nearly knocking Marie flat, and a vision entered:

long golden hair, enormous eyes, and a tiny skirt with legs that went on for ever and ever with Doc Martens on the feet of 'em. After her came a small man with two large bulgy men behind him.

'Daddy!' shrieked the rainbow vision.

'Who are you?' Dad asked nervously.

The vision pushed Marie out of the way and grabbed Dad, kissing him over and over again.

'Let go,' he yelled. 'Stop, stop all this. Stop kissing me, for Pete's sake. I'm covered in lipstick . . . Who are you?'

'It's Sharon, of course,' Mum snapped. Ems started to howl. Marie picked her up, glaring at Sharon, who moved off Dad and on to Mum and began all over again.

'That's enough,' ordered Mum. 'Whatever's going on?'

'Don't kiss me neither,' I yelled.

'Last time I saw you,' shouted Dad, 'you looked like a cross between an out-of-work rock star and a coal miner. What happened? And who are those men propping up the doorway? Gangsters?'

'Dad, Mum, everybody . . . Oh! It's wonderful you're here, Dad, to hear the marvellous news,' screamed Sharon. 'Meet my husband.'

'Who?' cried Mum.

'What?' cried Dad.

'Where?' I yelled.

'It's him, innit, Sharon,' Marie said, pointing at Director Boss man Blue Stubble, who was smiling at us all. The two bulgy men smiled as well and leaned forward a bit more, filling up the doorway.

'You've all got to congratulate me!' shrieked Sharon. 'I've come specially back here to tell my lovely family. All the way from New York . . .'

'You've caused us a lot of worry and bother,' my mum said, 'not telling us where you were. We've nearly had the police out, you know. I thought you were with Marshy, but I was still worried. It wasn't much fun for us . . .'

Sharon took no notice. She'd never taken much notice of any of us.

'We're married. I'm rich. And I'm going to be a star. Aren't I, Maxi darling?'

'You are a star, dearest Bubblekin,' he said.

'Let me out of this bloomin' hall!' shouted Dad. 'I think I'm going mad. I need air.'

'Let's all have a nice cup of tea,' said Mum.

'No. Champagne. Bring in the crates. Lads!' Blue Stubble snapped his fingers. The doorstops straightened up and things began to happen at the front and outside. 'Wake up the street.

Champagne and treats for everybody!'

'Just call me Max,' he said as we headed back into the kitchen.

Marie sat on the stairs and stared at Blue Stubble. She looked gobsmacked.

'You're my brother now!'

'That's right.'

'We haven't got enough glasses,' Mum said.

'Not to worry. They're on the way! Hurry it up, lads!'

The street was going to have its party after all. Wow! WOW! DOUBLE WOW!! AND TRIPLE WOW!!! FIREWORKS! CELEBRATIONS! STREET BANDS! KARAOKE! BUBBLY! A GOOD TIME FOR ALL!

Four

Down the hall and into the kitchen came the crates of champagne.

'That stuff costs a fortune,' cried Dad, looking at the labels.

'He's got a fortune,' grinned Sharon.

'Costs a bomb,' echoed Slug.

'He's probably got some of those as well,' hissed Marie.

'Don't you like him, Marie?'

'You can say that again.'

'Well, I don't like Sharon much. Even if she is my sister,' I whispered, and then everything went mad as corks popped and fizz flew everywhere.

'Oooh! Ooh!' Ems shrieked, chasing the bubbles. Down the hall and into the kitchen came trays of food, balloons, decorations, squeakers. Tables, umbrellas, streamers, flags, sweets and drinks all appeared in the house and in the street as if by magic. The rain held off.

'It wouldn't dare rain with *him* about,' Marie muttered.

'Oooh! Ooh! Ooh!' shrieked Ems, even louder.

Through the hall came people, hundreds of them, people from our street, people with telly faces that you know but don't know, reporters and camera people.

'I knew there weren't enough glasses,' groaned Mum.

Max lifted Sharon on to the kitchen table.

'The most beautiful bride in the world,' somebody called out.

She held out her hands for hush. 'They offered me the Ritz, but I knew it just had to be here. In my old home, in my old kitchen, in our street, the centre of my life and my love till now . . .'

'That's funny,' Mum put in. 'I can't remember you doing anything at all except grumble and gripe when you lived here.'

Slug and me crammed our plates with food.

'Luscious!'

'Brilliant!'

'Scrumptious!'

'Great!'

'Grab some cola as well, Slug!'

'This is fun. This is special.'

What Slug grabbed didn't taste much like cola, but it was very nice so we drank it and then some more. And more.

Cameras whirred and blinked and did whatever they do.

'Speech! Speech! Magnus! Sharon!'

Sharon smiled and smiled.

'Call me Max,' smiled Magnus.

'Lovely, lovely Rose of Sharon!'

'Speech!'

'I'm so happy,' she cried. 'Aren't we, Maxi darling?'

'We're so happy,' Maxi darling cried.

Old Mrs Birkinshaw, who was filling up a large part of the kitchen, started to sing, 'No two people have ever been so in love, been so in love, been so in love . . .'

'I'll have to get her into a chair before she has one of her turns,' said Mum, moving over.

Things were hotting up now, everyone eating, drinking, singing or swaying. The house rocked.

'The new face of the twenty hundreds!' cried somebody.

'She isn't twenty,' corrected Slug. 'She's sixteen.'

'You old enough to be married?' asked a man, young, OK.

'Of course I am. I just like older men,' snapped Sharon.

'You'll need to. He's well over forty and he's had at least five other wives already.'

Sharon grinned – a grinny grin, this time.

'I know that. What about *you* minding your own business?'

She called over to Blue Stubble, 'Maxi darling?'

Maxi darling looked at one of the bulgy men and then the young man had to leave quickly, helped on from behind. Ems had found the other bulgy man and stretched out her arms to be lifted. We waited for the yell as she patted his face and he almost smiled. It soon came.

'Ooowwwww! You horror!'

'Don't hurt her!' cried Max.

'She hurt me. Nearly bit me ear off.'

He was bleeding. Ems smiled happily. Mum left Mrs Birkinshaw and mopped up the minder.

'Tell us, tell us all about the wedding!' shouted someone.

Reporters had notebooks out. Camcorders whirred.

'Bring the grub under the table,' I told Slug. 'They won't tread on us under there.'

We made a cave. Good, it was. I was feeling a bit wuzzy by now. Probably the noise. I drank some more of the cola that tasted different. It fizzed in my nose.

'We got married in New York and then we honeymooned in the States. The Deep South. Magnolias. *Gone with the Wind*,' Sharon was saying. 'Oh! Oh! Oh! I can't begin to tell you . . .'

'Don't bother,' yelled Marie. 'We don't much want to know.'

'Southern nights and southern skies.' She hummed a few bars. 'Then I came back to see my dear old dad and mum and Marie and Gary, and little David, our friend.'

'Didn't know I was her friend,' Slug said.

Sharon was still talking. Her voice had changed.

'She's so phoney,' Marie muttered.

'She's like the weather. Changes all the time,' I said, which was true. Sharon had changed from being a top-of-the-class swot into a road protester and now into a rich celebrity bitch, I thought.

'Yes. Lots of projects,' Sharon was saying. 'We're teeming with ideas. We're off to the

Castle first. That's Maxi's other project, you know, as well as films. Moors and forests for miles. Away from all the stress and bustle of life here. We are busy hauling it all into the twenty-first century. Maxi's creating the biggest theme park in the world. Aren't you, Maxi darling?'

'Yes, my dreamboat.'

Long pause.

'They're snogging,' Slug muttered.

Cheers went up and shouts of 'More! More! More Mr and Mrs Moore!'

'Here comes the bride, short, fat and wide,' I sang.

'Shut up, Gary.'

'Nobody'll hear me in all this racket.'

'And then what are you doing? Modelling? Singing? Getting an album together? Writing a novel?' someone asked.

'When the theme park's really off the ground I'm starring in a musical of *Pride and Prejudice*.'

'I know, you're Lydia, the one who runs away and gets married?'

'No, I'm Elizabeth. The one who marries Mr Darcy, the richest man of the lot.'

'Yeah, that'd fit Sharon,' said Marie, joining us under the table.

'Well, she could be squatting in some old

dump with a penniless bloke or up in the trees with Marshy as Tarzan and her as Jane. At least this one's rich.'

'So everybody keeps saying.'

'Lovely, lovely Rose of Sharon,' sang out somebody.

'We could turn that into a hit,' yelled a guy with specs and stubble even bluer than Magnus Moore's.

'Belt up,' muttered Marie.

'All the family are coming to live with Magnus at his Castle,' somebody announced.

'Not if I can help it,' Dad shouted.

At that moment Ems crawled under the table just as Slug threw up all over us.

I don't really remember much more. When I came to I was in bed and it was tomorrow.

Five

They said the street party went on till next day, when Magnus and Sharon departed in a silver Porsche to London.

Sharon hit the headlines: 'Tree Girl Climbs to Top of the Tree' and 'Rose of Sharon Flies to the Moon' and 'Sweet Sixteen Is the Face Of Two Thousand' and 'A Face in a Thousand! No! A Face in Two Thousand!'

'Whatta loada rubbish,' I said to Slug when Marie showed us some.

'She looks lovely, though, in the pictures,' he sighed. 'You wouldn't know her now, would you?'

'I never knew her anyway,' I said. 'Not really.'

After Dad had pushed yet another photographer down our steps, he said he'd had enough and was off back to his oil rig.

'I'd rather have the North Sea any day,' he told the next bunch of press men. 'My family are great, but I'm a man for peace and quiet.'

They shot questions at him.

'No, I don't want to work for Moore's enterprises, thank you very much,' he answered. 'I've always bin able to earn enough to take care of me and mine and I intend keeping it that way.'

He said goodbye to us all in the kitchen, where you couldn't be spotted because of the blind over the window.

Ems clung to him like chewing gum. She'd decided she loved him.

'Dad-Dad!' she screamed. 'Dad-Dad!'

'Just fancy. Her first word,' smiled Slug sloppily.

Dad threw her up in the air.

'You're like a mad pixie,' he cried, and they both shrieked with laughter. He shook hands with me and Slug.

'Keep your eye on things,' he told Marie.

'I am doing. I'm making a scrapbook and keeping a diary.'

'Well, tell your mother I'm off and she's not to worry.'

Mum had been called to Mrs Birkinshaw, who'd had another of her turns.

'Ta-ta, kids,' and Dad was gone, out the back door, through the garden and down the alleyway while Marie leaned out of the front window shouting, 'I can see my sister coming down the road in that red car.'

Then she slammed the window shut.

'Pity the folk in the red car,' Slug said, as the photographers rushed after it.

Marie settled down with her scrapbook.

'Have you stuck in all Sharon's pictures yet?' I asked.

'Not yet. But look at what I *have* cut out.'

A consignment of fresh wild animals has arrived at Magnus Moore's theme park . . .

'And this. Very interesting.'

In small print at the bottom of the back page was:

Nothing further has been heard of Polly Sims, the journalist, who has gone missing without trace.

'What are you thinking, Marie?'

'Not thinking anything.'

She opened the sideboard and fished out her money box and started counting. Three pounds and sixty-four pence and a foreign coin. 'Keep your mitts off it,' she shouted.

'What you saving for, Marie? We're supposed to be rich now, ain't we?'

'Are we? Sharon may be rich. Dad's got a good job, but we're as poor as ever.'

'Well, what you saving for? A video?'

'Dunno. Yes, I do. A crisis.'

'What's a crisis?'

'Oh, y'know. A dang'rous moment in your life.'

'What dang'rous moment?'

'I dunno. Stop pestering me.'

And off she went. To see Katy Simmons two doors away, now WPC Simmons in the police force. She was a family friend who used to look after Marie when she was little. And me and Slug, sometimes.

'Take Ems with you, please. Me and Slug don't want to look after her.'

'OK.' Marie dumped her in the buggy, fastened her in, shook it and said, 'Don't you dare get out.'

And off they went out the back way just as Mum arrived fighting her way in the front.

'Go away!' she cried to the crowd. 'He's gone. She's gone. No need to stay. Nothing will happen now. Go home. Leave us alone.'

She flopped down on the sofa.

'What's up, Mum?'

'Oh, nothing really. Except I shall miss your

father. And Sharon being a slob all round the place. Funny I miss her, but I do.'

'She's rich now, Mum. Perhaps we'll be rich too.'

'Fat chance. And I don't want his money anyway. I wanted Sharon to get her A-levels and go to university. I didn't mind her being a traveller with Marshy now and then in the holidays, but I didn't want her to be – a – Barbie Doll! A Barbie Doll with Doc Marten boots!'

What could we say?

'I like Barbie Dolls,' sighed Slug sadly.

'Mum, can we 'ave some money to spend at the corner shop?'

'Yes, go on. Enjoy yourselves.'

So we did.

One misty morning it slid into the street, a long, long black car. We were already packed, even Mum. Max had phoned two days ago, telling us to get ready to stay at Moore Castle, where parties and rides and excitement and EVERYTHING waited for us. Sharon would be there and Max himself – and they hoped to get Dad to join us.

'He won't come,' Mum said. 'And I don't want to.'

'Oh, please, Mum.'

'Mum, you ought to. You'll see Sharon. Come wiv us. Please.'

'All right, then. For you lot. But I'd rather stay here at home, really.'

So there we were. Bags packed, we stood in the hall all ready as the long, long black car parked in front of most of the houses and cars in the street. The driver rang the bell, but stayed outside. He was giant-sized, like the car.

'No one,' he announced to the street kids all coming round to look, 'is going to strip the tyres, scratch the paintwork, pinch the television or anything else. I carry a special ray gun and the car will electrocute you in two seconds if I press this button on this ring I wear. See?'

The kids moved back. The photographers zoomed near. Ems beamed and stretched up to him, patting him.

'Dad-Dad,' she cooed. We all piled in, Mum last.

And there came a cry from next door.

'Come. Come, Nellie! Quick! You're wanted. She's having a really bad one and wants you.'

Mrs Birkinshaw had struck again. The driver pulled away. 'Nearly got that one,' he shouted as a photographer leapt out of the way just in time. So we ended up on our own, travelling to Moore Castle without Mum.

'Marie, Marie,' cried Mum as we pulled away. 'Look after Ems for me.'

'What about me?' I cried, but we were already too far away for her to hear.

Six

So there we were – Marie, Slug, Ems and me in a car the size of Buckingham Palace travelling who-knows-where with three people we didn't know and didn't much want to know from the look of them, the enormous chauffeur and right in the back, behind the curtains, another minder and a woman with a face like a drain cover. It was all a bit much. Mum ought to have come wiv us. But then Drain Cover reached out for Ems, murmuring something about a lovely little girl, though how she could tell beat me as Ems mostly looks like ET. Anyway, Ems kicked her and crawled on to the Minder who was big and black and bald and ugly as well as bulgy.

'Dad-Dad,' she shrieked and kissed him, patting his bulges. He looked terrified.

'Take her off me, somebody!'

'Dad-Dad,' cried Ems, holding him tight. 'Ni . . . Dad-Dad!'

'She's said another word. I think it was

"nice",' Slug beamed. 'Gary, Gary, she's starting to talk.'

'So what?' I answered. There were loads of buttons and I was busy pressing them. A TV screen shot into view, rock music belted out, a drinks table shot up, the car blinds rolled up and down like crazy, the lights came on and little trays of crisps, nuts and raisins whirled out everywhere.

'A James Bond-mobile. Gadgets galore!' cried Marie. 'I wonder if it's got machine guns on the front and back and smokescreens as well.'

'Can I try them? Please. Please,' I cried.

'Just you leave things alone!' snapped Mrs Drain Cover. She wasn't murmuring gently any more.

The minder made a growly noise deep in his throat. Ems patted him to see where it came from.

'Dad-Dad-Dad-Dad-Dad!'

'Gerrer off me,' he shouted. 'She terrifies me.' He tried to push Ems away. She wailed loudly.

'Remember we're to take great care of them,' Drain Cover snapped at him.

'Come on, Ems,' said Marie, and she climbed

obediently on to her lap where she helped herself to crisps. So did the rest of us.

'I'm Mrs Harris and I'm your nanny while you're with us for this lovely holiday,' said Mrs Drain Cover. 'This is Martin the Minder and that's Dennis the Driver. He also helps look after the wild animals in the park.'

'Should let him look after Ems, then,' I said, as I fiddled about. 'She's like a wild animal.'

'No, don't open the partition, Gary – is it? Just leave it . . .'

'I want to sit by the driver.'

'Leave the partition *alone*, boy. Oh, Marie, is it? Try to stop the wee one throwing crisps and nuts everywhere. Yes, you may have some Coke or fruit juice and there are comics and magazines to read. All laid out specially for your comfort. As long as you behave yourselves . . .'

'I want to sit at the front wiv 'im,' I cried.

'SIT STILL, I TELL YOU,' cried Drain Cover. 'Now, this is what we've planned for you. It's a long journey but we shall stop half-way at a motorway service station – where I trust you'll behave. . . . And we should arrive at Moore's Magic Castle at nightfall, where you'll have your supper and go to bed. Then tomorrow you'll meet Mr Magnus Moore and we'll outline the wonderful programme laid on ready for you. Anything to say?'

Slug, who had been very quiet for some time, opened his mouth to say, 'Sorry. I'm gonna be sick.'

And he was. All over the drinks and the beautiful seats and cream carpet and Minder Martin's shoes. He howled out loud, 'That's it. I'm handing in my notice!'

'How are you back there?' asked Dennis, opening up the partition.

'Stop, stop!' cried Nanny Harris. 'You horrible, disgusting children!'

'Can't stop here. Motorway,' yelled Dennis.

'Slug's always sick. He's got a weak stomach,' I tried to explain.

'That's it. I'm leaving,' repeated Minder Martin.

'You can't! Remember your contract,' warned Nanny Harris.

'I can't stand this. This isn't my sort of life,' wailed Minder Martin. 'I hate kids!'

'SHUT UP! EVERYBODY QUIET! *You*, drive on to the hard shoulder, stop and I'll deal with it.' It was Marie speaking.

And she did deal with it. She always does. I

told you she's wonderful. But she made me do the most messy bits.

'I hate you, Slug,' I said, then he began to cry. So I said, 'No, I don't. Just shut up.'

The journey went on for ever after we'd been cleaned up. We stopped at the motorway service station and then drove on and on again. I woke up later to find I'd been sleeping on Blah, Ems's hideous teddy with no eyes or ears. Then I went off to sleep again.

When I came to, we were driving along a narrow road, trees on both sides, woods so thick they darkened the car. And these woods stretched on as far as I could see. The road twisted and turned, rose up and down, up and down, and round hairpin bends. *Whoosh*, we splashed through a stream. And on we drove through the night. I didn't know there was so much country. Miles and miles of country.

Knackered from sitting, I just wanted to get there. Soon, please. This place was a thousand miles away from home. A thousand years from the street. Light years away from Mum. She didn't care. She should've come. She shouldn't've left Ems and us with this Nanny Drain Cover. I was afraid, chicken. I wanted Dad, big, hairy Dad. I didn't like Nanny Harris, nor the Minder. And where was Sharon? Even Sharon would be *something*.

Marie poked me. I looked at her. Her eyes were shining, her cheeks pink. Her hair glowed.

'Look, Gary. Oh, look! Isn't it brill? Triffic! Fantastic! There could even be wolves or bears out there. Or giants or ogres or pixies or – DANGER! Oh, Gary, it's an *adventure*, innit? Oh, Gary! A real live adventure!'

Part Two

One

I couldn't move my legs.

My legs were trapped.

Trapped in oozy, squelchy, stinking mud.

Mud bubbling and seething, sucking me down, down, dragging me into this rotten, skanky swamp, with giant green monster leaves hanging all around, around, around and into it – awful, horrible, beastly plants and mud all out to get me, eat me alive, swallow me up – no more Gary . . . ow . . . help, please!

I saw a warty branch hanging over my head and clutched at it but a forked tongue flickered, a python slithered and twined along the branch towards me, wicked slitty eyes glittering into mine.

'Marie! Marie! Marie! Save me! Save . . . !' Scream, scream, scream!

And I woke up out of that gross, stinking mud, rising up and up until I was gazing at a pointed sky above, glittering . . . but not with snake eyes . . . With stars.

43

Where was I? 'Help! HELP! It's *me*, Gary! Help!'

I was in a strange bed, pulling and tugging at the duvet, screaming and shouting, but no sound coming out. A strange bed, a strange room, a strange place. What was I doing here? Crazy, crazy.

Long black limo, Marie, Slug – Slug being sick, always being sick, me asleep with Blah, Ems on the big black bloke, Nanny Harris with a face like a drain-cover, Driver Dennis driving for miles . . . feeling excited at first, then bored, tired, travelling on through miles of woods and narrowing into lanes with grass growing down the middle, owls hooting, the car going bum-petty bumpetty, *Another badger done for*, mutters Minder – Minder what? – Minder Martin, Marie shouting how horrible, how sad, poor badger, splashing through a ford, wow, gates opening, a long, long gravelly drive going through trees to a castle black against the night sky, Marie shout-ing 'It's magic, look, look – a drawbridge, a moat – look, look, Gary, Slug, Ems, wake up, we're here!'

A huge hall with lights that dazzled. Supper at a long table. Bed. I didn't remember getting into bed. Somebody must've undressed me. Hope it wasn't Nanny Drain Cover. Far away I could hear Marie saying, 'What a wonderful, magic, strange room . . .'

But – the swamp. I didn't like that swamp and the snake. What I wanted now was my own room wiv posters of Arsenal and Aston Villa and Newcastle on the walls and old roller skates, and heaps of grot and sweaty socks under the bed and the Terminator and an old picture of the Flopsy Bunnies.

I felt horrible. Nanny Drain Cover probably drugged that warm drink last night and that's why I felt so grotty. Sharon's rotten old wrinkly, Blue Stubble, was gonna sell us for slaves. That's the answer. That's it. That's how he's got all that money, drugging kids and selling them for slaves to big fat men wearing robes round their bellies and teacloths on their bonces. Bet Slug won't fetch much. He'll be past his sell-by date, though Slug's been past his sell-by date from the day he was born, or even his give-away date. And at the thought of Slug, *Zzzzzzzzzhhhhhhhhhh.*

Zzzzzzzzzhhhhhhhhhh. Like an ogre snoring in a dark room.

I pushed back the duvet and sat upright. Slug had started to snore his head off. There he lay in a little bed next to mine, snoring like a brick rattling in a cement mixer. 'Stop it, won't ya!'

It was getting lighter, though stars still shone through the pointy window and I could see clearly now a ceiling that rose into a point covered with gold and silver stars – a fairy-tale room (for Marie) or a room for nightmare tales floating on a swamp – Go away, snake, go away, swamp – for always.

Zzzzzzzzzhhhhhhhhhh.

Zzzzzzzzzhhhhhhhhhh.

Why doesn't that stupid git belt up? 'Shut up, Slug,' I hissed. 'I hate you.'

I could see we were sleeping in a round room – must be a tower or a turret, weird, with Slug near and Marie opposite with Ems next to her in a cot.

Zzzzzzzzzhhhhhhhhhh.

And there was a door next to Ems. Why's that? Just then a figure came out of it. Must be another room there. I didn't dare move . . .

SUPPOSE IT WAS COMING TO KILL US ALL!

Then I thought at least it'll stop Slug snoring, and saw that it was Nanny Drain Cover Harris stomping over to Slug's bed. I didn't dare move as she turned him over on to his side, muttering and grumbling. He stopped snoring with a gynormous snort that nearly shot me out of bed, loud enough to wake all the castle ghosts, and there must be hundreds in this place – if ever there was a ghost place this was it – then she tramped back to the door in the wall, her room, I supposed.

Sleep was a good idea. I snuggled down, then sat up again as I thought of something. Yeah, yeah, I'd guessed right. Only one door out of here and that led into Nanny Drain Cover's pad. To get out you'd have to go through her room. We were prisoners, sort of – huh! Knackered now, I curled up and shut my eyes – Go away, snake, go away swamp. Don't come near me. Think about playing for England and scoring a hat-trick, one, two, three, Gary, Gary, Gary, hooray, Gary's the Greatest . . .

Zzzzzzzzzhhhhhhhhhh.
Zzzzzzzzzhhhhhhhhhh.

In a black rage I leapt out of bed, hit Slug and shoved him off his back. Silence. At last. Back to my own bed.

Zzzzzzzzzhhhhhhhhhh.
Zzzzzzzzzhhhhhhhhhh.

Duvet over head. No difference. His snores would bore through any duvet.

47

'I'll kill him,' I said to the stars shining through the window. 'I really will. I'll kill him!' I cried to the stars painted on the ceiling.

A voice came from Marie's bed.

'David. Now go to sleep, there's a good boy. And stop snoring.'

Like toothache stopping, silence slid gently into the turret room, for Slug always, always, always does what Marie tells him.

Two

'Gary, you mindless, brain-dead twit, come
and look! Look! It's like a map! It's my magic,
alternative world!'

Marie was leaning out of the pointy windows,
holding up Ems to look, Slug peering and
squinting and hopping beside her.

'Look! Look!'

'I will if Slug shifts his big bonce!'

'Like a medieval map!'

'Eh?'

'The old history maps looked like that. All laid
out before us, the hills over there, the woods, the
water, the little railway, the entertainment
park . . .'

'I hate you, Slug!'

'Gary! Stop it! Look at this fantastic view . . .'

'Gary! Why you hitting me?'

'Stop it, Gary! Don't be so GROSS! Don't
cry, David. Gary, leave him alone and look at
this view, this place. Max, I love you. Just fancy,
he's our brother now. We're so lucky! To be here

with all this. Look at all those roller-coasters and the animals – the animals in the enclosures – look, Ems, there's an elephant! You'll be able to see an elephant and maybe a lion! Oh, Ems, I wanted magic and I've got it. Oh, won't it be wonderful? I'll speak to every animal. I'll go on every roller-coaster, Nemesis, Oblivion, Black-Hole and Bullet. Oh, we're the luckiest kids in all the world. Disneyland's nothing compared to this! Gary! Gary! Say something!'

'Yeah. It's OK. I wish *he* didn't *snore.*'

'Oh, forget it. Ems . . .'

She was covering Ems with kisses. Ems pushed her off and rubbed her face.

'Let's get dressed and get out there!'

High as a kite, Marie jumped and sang. This is how she gets, she doesn't need drugs or anything. It's her nature. She seized Slug and made him dance like a hopping toad round the room to one of the songs she makes up, she's always making up songs . . .

> *'Maxi's the greatest,*
> *Maxi's the latest*
> *Guy in the world*
> *He's so neat*
> *He's so sweet . . .'*

'Come along, wee kiddies. It's brekky time for bibbies.'

Nanny Harris was smiling – a nasty sight – though not as bad as Marie singing. Was I gonna wake up to this every morning? I sure was gonna miss my room with its treasures in it.

'Come along! Chop, chop!' cried Nanny Drain Cover. 'Let's see who can be first, shall we?'

I sat on the bed, deciding to be last – but then I did really want to see this place, the castle and all the park, so I started to get dressed.

Nanny Drain Cover stopped smiling. She'd picked up Ems to dress her and was holding something pink and frilly.

'You ought to hev a nice, sweet, pretty dress,' she said, 'and then you'd look a dear wee girlie. Try this on and we'll see what we can do . . . Ow!'

Ems bit her and ran round and round the room.

'She won't wear that thing,' Marie said. 'You're wasting your time.'

Nanny Drain Cover caught up with Ems at last. 'You notty thing – bad gurrlie. Didn't your mother teach you better manners?'

I put my tongue out at her. 'Leave my mother out of this. And go away while I get dressed.'

'Ye see what I mean? I'll have to poot some work in on all of you so as to be fit to be in this wonderful castle, fit for a princess. Who'd a thought the lovely Sharon would have a family like you lot o' heathens.' She sniffed. 'So scruffy. So common!'

'Push off, you ole bag!' I yelled. 'It's bad enough sharing a room wiv all this crowd and 'im snoring all night long wivout you for breakfast on top of it.'

'Calm down, everybody. Let's go and eat,' smiled Marie, so we got dressed and after a while we set off in search of grub.

Downstairs – and there were dozens of stairs down in this castle – we went like a procession, with me coming last. Out of nowhere a pretty girl appeared and smiled at me.

'You're Gary, aren't you? Hungry?'

I nodded.

'Just follow that smell. Oh, have a nice day! And . . . Gary – take care, won't you?'

'What you mean?'

'Oh, lots of danger about in an adventure theme park, Gary – rides and things. And wild animals. Good luck. Have a nice day!'

And she'd gone.

There was a double door ahead with brass knobs on – made for a giant. Nanny Drain Cover pushed it open. We were in a room bigger than our street. You could have roasted a hairy mammoth in the fireplace at the far end.

The table down the centre of the room was longer than a mile. The walls around were covered with carved beasts, gargoyles, monsters, the ceiling hung above us a million miles away and was covered with everything – faces, nasties, angels, stars and shields. It was all a bit much for me. I could see Slug's face everywhere in the carvings.

The never-ending sideboard had the lot – oranges, bananas, kiwis, mangoes, bacon, twenty different cereals, eggs, sausages, fried potatoes, black-pudding, beans, tomatoes, mushrooms, honey, jam, marmalade, hot bread, black bread, brown bread, speckly bread, toast, croissants, biscuits, kippers.

'Just dig in.'

Ems had spotted Minder Martin and hauled herself on to his knee. She started to feed him with what he'd got on his plate. His face was a picture, painted in food.

I started to feel better. Forget swamps, snakes and Slug. Things could be OK.

Ems threw a bowl of cereal that Nanny Drain Cover had given her on the floor. Minder Martin picked it up, not easy with his figure. She threw it down again.

'Don't hate me, Gary,' pleaded Slug through the sausage he was spreading with strawberry jam.

'You can go on living. But watch it, mate.'

Three

Crash! Wham! Splatter! Bash! Bang! Wallop! –
straight into the side of Slug's green dodgem. He
spun round and round, sparks flying all around
the car, sparks round the rubber, sparks in the
air, disco music belting in our ears, throbbing,
blasting. Twisting and turning I smashed into
him again and again. I'd teach him to snore at
me in the night. It must have been that which
gave me that stinking slime nightmare. Singing
and shouting, I rushed at him again. He seemed
to be yelling, 'Cool it, Gary.' I didn't care. This
was great, this was fun, this was fantastic. I was
high as a kite, mad as a hatter. Corkscrews, Big
Wheels, Roller-Coasters, Black Holes, I love 'em
all, but dodgem cars are best . . . Give me a
dodgem car and I'm a Formula One racing
driver, the best, the greatest in the world –
Number One Ace, Gary, the star, the Wonder
Man. I saw off Slug and turned on Marie – who
does she think she is? Some sort of alien ruler?
the Queen? the Prime Minister? Wallop to you,

Marie, and you, Slug. Bang! Crash! Wham!

And then the bloke turned off the power.

'You've had long enough, mates,' he cried.

But that was later.

Earlier in the morning, after we'd finally finished eating breakfast, Nanny Drain Cover Harris said, 'Follow me, children,' in an I-hate-you-but-I've-been-told-to-do-this voice and we went after her into the courtyard where a zip-around four-by-four was parked.

'I thought we were looking round the park.'

'You are. But it's a fair size, if you hadn't noticed.' She pointed down the endless drive which stretched as far as the eye could see.

'Still, if you'd like to walk, I've brought the buggy for the wee one.'

For one crazy moment I thought Marie was going to say yes.

'No, you drive us there, please.' She smiled sweetly, Marie the Creep, making up for the rest of us.

We drove out of the courtyard through a sort of spiked gate, a portcullis, said Marie, they let it down to keep out their enemies and they pulled up the drawbridge so they'd have to swim the moat.

The moat looked deep and murky as we drove over it and past gardens to the drive lined with dozens of trees like soldiers. And then the car stopped at a little station where a miniature train was waiting.

'There's no one about yet. I thought crowds came here,' said Marie.

'It's airly yet. The park won't be open for the public,' she sniffed, ''till ten o'clock. But you can go round. Sir Magnus has laid it all on especially for you wee bairns. I cain't imagine why.'

'*Sir* Magnus?'

'Yes, he's been knighted for his services to British Films.'

'*So*. That means Sharon's a *Lady*,' Marie spoke very slowly.

'Indeed, yes. And as part of a lady's family you all should behave' – sniff – 'well.'

'Lady Muck,' I muttered, 'is more like it.'

'That's quaite enough, Gary. Perhaps your mither will think to send you to a school where they will teach you propair manners when you go back home. And now you catch the train here and it'll take you round the park to see the animals. I can come with you if you like but I'm sure you children would rather go on your own. You can look after them, can't you?' she added to Marie. 'And there are others around who can help if you need it. Plenty of others.'

'Course I can,' said Marie. Me and Slug agreed as well. We wanted to be with Drain Cover about as much as she wanted to be with us.

'I love trains,' said Slug, who hadn't been on many. Nor me.

'It's cute,' said Marie, looking at the empty open-air carriages and engine blowing steam into the air. We got out of the car and Nanny Drain Cover drove away quickly, glad to get away.

'Jump aboard then, kids,' said a man sitting behind the engine. We sat at the back of the train facing one another as it chugged away slowly at first, then gathered speed as we chuffed through a tunnel and down to a lake, disturbing a flock of pink flamingos. Ems pointed to them and made gooey sounds.

'Look! Look!' cried Slug, nudging me as we passed a paddock in which zebra and gazelles were grazing together.

'Push off, Slug.' I wanted to kick him, a feeling I often had.

The train left the lake and pulled out into a wide flat area where rhinoceros and giraffes and elephants could be seen roaming. One giraffe came near, its long neck bent down, and Ems tried to jump off the train to get on to it. She must've thought it was a long slide or something.

Then the track became more overgrown with thick bushes on either side and the train began to pull upwards. Looking out into the trees I saw another animal, looking weird, like a man in green. I squinted against the sun to see it more clearly, but it scurried away into a bush out of sight. I must've imagined it, but it seemed real.

'What was that?' I asked, but Marie and Slug hadn't seen it.

Notices with 'Dangerous Animals: Keep Out!' appeared. Leopards lay on tree branches, lions lazed in heaps flat out and a couple of Siberian tigers paced, full of menace. It was weird to see them in the countryside instead of sheep and cows.

Into the tiger enclosure a white shadow emerged like a ghost and joined the other tigers, then another one appeared.

'Look at those two,' Marie cried. 'White tigers! They're the most beautiful of all.'

'And the fiercest, I bet,' I said. 'I think they're scary.'

One of them saw me and looked me straight in

the eye as if it was trying to tell me something. I shivered, not from cold. I knew I was safe enough here on the train, but those eyes would scare anyone anywhere. What was it thinking? Did it want to eat me? Did it hate this strange place it was stuck in?

'Tyger! Tyger! Burning bright,' Marie murmured.

'You're right, for once,' I answered.

Then the huge form of Dennis the Driver appeared, cleaning out one of the cages.

'Bet the animals are too scared to attack him!'

Soon afterwards the train slowed down and finally came to a halt. 'OK, then, folks,' the man said. 'Here's where you get off.'

Spread out as far as we could see were multi-coloured rides, dodgems, chutes, raft rides, space rides, octopuses, big wheels, everything. In the background were shops, and cages for the smaller animals. Beyond that again building materials were scattered and piled up in great heaps. Where the builders were working was all fenced off. 'No trespassers'.

'Look, they've got one of those water-chute rides,' Marie yelled. 'Come on, Gary!'

'No, no! The dodgem cars! My favourite!' I

yelled. 'D'you think they'll let us go on it?'

The man in charge grinned and said yes, it was OK. So we all piled on, Ems with Marie. I was plotting revenge on Slug the Useless and off we went, Crash! Wham! Spash! Bash! Bang! Wallop! Wow!

'Whizzer! Brill! Mega! Mega!' I shouted as we came off. 'I'm gonna love it here!'

Marie sang:

> *'Maxi is the greatest,*
> *Maxi is our brother.*
> *He's made us rich,*
> *Given us all this,*
> *We don't want another!'*

'Here's to Sir Maxi Moore,' Slug joined in.

Ems banged Blah.

'Make him more Moor Moore!' screamed Marie.

We stopped to get our breath back and suddenly the pretty girl was with us, handing out drinks and ice-cream.

'What's your name?' I asked, feeling shy.

'Purdey Perdita,' she smiled at me. 'Have fun and a nice day.' She walked away.

'Perdita,' I whispered.

'Paradise must be like this,' Slug said.

'Shut up,' I answered automatically. 'We've hardly seen anything of it yet.'

We sat on the grass, drank our drinks and licked our ice-creams.

'Besides, I'm not sure this has much to do with paradise.' Marie's voice sounded a bit odd. 'Though, Gary . . .'

'Yeah?'

'D'you feel that – oh, I don't know how to say it – that someone's watching over us?'

'Don't be daft. Well, Brother Sir Maxi might be hovering in the sky above us or Nanny Drain Cover's an angel.'

We all fell about at this.

'C'mon, c'mon, then. What'll we go on next?' I asked.

'Let's try that,' said Marie, pointing to a ride shaped like a corkscrew.

'No way. I'm not going on that,' Slug protested. 'You and Gary do it. It scares me stupid.'

'That's 'cos you are,' I said.

Marie grabbed his arm and hauled him along. I followed. An assistant was standing there.

'Want a go?' he asked, opening the door on one of the cars.

'Yep,' said Marie.

'Yep,' I said.

'No,' said Slug. 'What about Ems?'

Marie glanced over at Ems asleep in her buggy and covered with ice-cream.

'She's OK for the minute. C'mon. You're scared, aren't you, David?'

'No, I'm not. I just don't want to go on it,' Slug said.

'You're a wimp. You're a wimp,' I taunted.

'Don't be horrible, Gary. You're always horrible to me.'

'That's 'cos you're you and I'm me,' I told him.

'Are you going on it or not?' asked the man.

'Yes, we are,' said Marie.

We got on, pushing each other. Slug didn't move. 'I'll just watch you two for the minute,' he said.

'Oh, you chicken,' I said.

'Well, you look after Ems, then,' said Marie.

'OK. If she wakes up I'll take her over there.' He pointed to a bouncy castle near the shops.

As if she'd been listening, Ems woke up and banged Blah up and down. She gurgled happily, a good sign. If she wasn't happy you soon knew

63

about it. So they pushed off towards the bouncy castle.

'Slug won't go on anything high,' Marie whispered as we waited for the machine to start. 'He gets vertigo.'

'What?'

'Oh, Gary. Don't always be so thick! He gets dizzy if he goes up high.'

'Well, he would, wouldn't he? Wimp! Hey, I can see a virtual reality machine. They're really cool, Marie. You should have a go.'

'Later. We're off! Hey!'

The Corkscrew started to move and went into a series of loops, followed by one corkscrew, then another, up and down, in and out. As the G-forces took over my stomach rose and fell, my head spun, I was turned inside out, upside down, twisted round and round, heart in my mouth, spaced out, totally gone, not knowing where I was, but hearing Marie's shrieks with mine as we zoomed at fantastic speed. Little bits of the park whirled round far below me, then as the machine started to slow down it came back more into focus. Finally it ground to a halt. Wow! What an experience!

'That was absolutely brill. Let's have another go,' said Marie.

'Yeah. That was wicked,' I said. 'But wait –'

I could see Slug running towards us – with an empty pushchair.

'What's happened? He's shouting! Listen.'

'Ems! Ems!' wept Slug. 'She's disappeared.'

Four

'Marie,' Slug shouted. 'Marie, Marie. Come quick! Ems has gone.' He was in tears.

'Useless git,' I muttered. 'Can't you do anythin' right?'

'Well, let's find her then. She can't have gone far.'

Marie asked the man from the ride if he'd seen her, but he shook his head and it was then panic hit us – knowing Ems, she could be anywhere, doing anything. We searched and searched through the amusement park. No joy. No Ems.

'She might have gone back to the bouncy castle,' said Slug. 'And the monkeys. We saw them on the way. She loved them. She kept making faces at them and one of them did the same back.'

I made a face at Slug, not a nice one.

'Hope you're right,' said Marie. 'Mum'll skin us alive if anything happens to her.'

We kept looking, but she still didn't turn up. I suddenly felt sick, Marie had turned white, Slug green. Behind the animal house and shops we came upon a maze with the challenging words, 'Be Warned! If You Enter This Maze It Will Take You at Least Half an Hour to Find Your Way Out!'

'Oh, no. She can't have gone in there,' I groaned.

'She can,' said Marie. 'We've looked everywhere round here.'

'Let's toss for who goes in,' said Slug, producing a coin.

'No way. We all go in together,' I said, 'or there'll be someone else beside Ems to look for. Anyway, you lost her, remember.'

'So you keep on reminding me,' moaned Slug. 'How many times do I have to say sorry?'

'Oh, shut up, you two,' said Marie. 'Let's go.'

We all entered the maze together. It was a pig – dead ends, high hedges, false trails. We seemed to be going round in circles, not getting anywhere.

'Stop!' yelled Marie, after hours, it seemed. 'We'll turn left at everything,' she commanded, always bossy-boots. Ages later we came out at the exit. It hadn't taken half an hour. It had taken an hour.

'She can't be in there,' I said. 'We must've gone over every inch of that maze.'

Slug started to cry again.

'Shut up! Crying's no good!'

'Let's go back to the castle,' said Marie. 'They'll send out people to look for her.'

'I hope the train's still there,' I groaned. 'The castle's miles away.'

Shrieks and roars came from the theme park as, knackered, we headed for the station. People had arrived. Then a roaring sound came from near by . . . and it wasn't people making that sound. No human being could.

'Oh, crikey! What's that?' gasped Slug.

'The lions. It's all right, they're all behind fences, ain't they?' said Marie.

'This one isn't!' I gibbered as we turned the corner and came face to face with it: a lion, a lion . . . A LION! Aaarhh!!!

Is this the end, I thought? If that lion wanted to eat me, I couldn't stop him. I couldn't even run. My legs had gone, turned to jelly.

I've told people what Marie's like and they don't believe me, but, cool as a cucumber, she went up to the lion and started to stroke his shaggy mane. He purred like a pet cat, a very large pet cat with a noisy engine . . .

'He's lovely,' she said. 'Come on, he won't hurt you.'

'I'll take your word for it, Marie.'

When I could bear to look I saw he was a manky old lion, scraggy and tatty looking. But he still scared me and Slug. We kept our distance as he and Marie gazed lovingly at each other.

'He might've eaten Ems,' I said, struck with new terror.

Marie bent down and looked in his mouth. The lion lifted up his great head to her.

'I don't think so. He's only got one tooth left.' She put her arms round his mane. 'We've got to go now. Don't hurt Ems if you see her. I love you, Joe Lion!'

Then the huge form of Dennis suddenly appeared. 'That's where you got to,' he said to the lion. 'Naughty creature, escaping while I was cleaning your cage.'

'He's – he's tame then, is he?' I asked him.

'Yeah, safe as houses. Got hardly any teeth or claws left to speak of. But can't have him wandering round scaring people, can we? C'mon, you, back to your home.'

We watched him as he escorted the lion away, then headed for the station again.

'I'd like to take him home as a pet,' said Marie.

'I'd like to see Mum's face if you did,' I said.

'And Dad would have a fit. He's not keen on pets anyway, let alone a bloomin' lion!'

Luckily the train was there. We all kept watch for Ems on the return journey, but she wasn't to be seen. Nor was Drain Cover with the car. Just the walk back up that long drive to the castle.

'I'll have to phone up Mum and tell her if we can't find Ems,' said Marie, sounding despairing at last.

'Well, don't say it was our fault,' I said. 'Slug lost her. Besides, we can live without her. She's been a nuisance ever since we got here.'

'Have you ever thought, Gary, that you are the most horrible boy in the world?'

'Yep. He is,' said Slug.

'So?' I answered. 'At least I'm not drippy like you two.'

Fed up, weary, knackered, we finally made it back to the castle.

And there in the courtyard was Minder Martin running round slowly and miserably. For on his shoulders he had Ems, who kept banging his head with Blah to make him go faster. He seemed glad to see us.

'Here's your kid sister,' he said, handing her to Marie.

'Thanks,' she gasped with relief. Even I was secretly pleased. Slug started to blub again.

'Where'd you find her?' I asked.

'I was drivin' round the estate when I found her bawling by the roadside and couldn't see you, so I brought her back here.' He paused, 'A long time ago.' He seemed as weary as we were.

'You naughty girl,' scolded Maric. Ems gurgled, then howled as Minder Martin disappeared.

'Want play more,' she screamed.

'She's talking. Ems is talking.' Slug's face turned purple with happiness.

That night I slept like a log, despite Slug's snoring. I think I could've slept through World War Three if that had started.

Five

At breakfast Ems headed for Minder Martin, who stood up and shouted, 'I've had enough of this. That kid'll drive me crazy. I'm leaving,' and headed for the door.

'And I don't see why *we* have to look after her. *She's* supposed to . . .' I pointed at Nanny Drain Cover.

Ems started to yell, and Marie picked her up. Didn't look like we were gonna have much of a day, but Pretty Girl Purdey suddenly stepped forward, took Ems and said, 'If somebody will look after my job for me, I'll look after Ems. You're gorgeous, aren't you?' And she tickled her tum, at which Ems shrieked, but with laughter this time. They sat down to eat breakfast and we got on with ours.

All the staff went into a huddle to sort things out and to fetch back Minder Martin or else Boss Man Max would be mad at them all.

'Where is Max, anyway?' asked Marie. 'Why

isn't he here looking after things? And where's my sister Sharon? What's she doing?'

'Yeah,' I added, not that I wanted to see either of 'em much, but it did seem peculiar that we'd been dumped here on our own. 'What they doin'?'

'Sir Max will be back with us this evening,' sniffed Nanny Harris, 'and her ladyship will be coming later. She's shopping in London at the moment.'

'Caw,' I said. What else? I got stuck into the grub instead of talking. At least we'd got rid of Ems for five minutes so we could watch the animals and go on rides in peace.

Which is what we did. We went on:

- the Bullet Ride on Flamingo Land
- the Play Station Ride
- Whirlitzer, Nemesis, Oblivion, Black Hole . . .

and then the Dodgems again as Slug was turning green. I was kind and didn't crash him too much. And then, a ride through the haunted tunnel with ghosts, ghouls, skellytons and monsters popping up everywhere. He liked that. Fellow feeling, I suppose.

*

73

People were filling the park now, and some were moving towards the fence beyond the animal enclosures where we were heading and on to the land where some building work was in progress.

'Something's happening,' said Marie.

'I can't see over the fence!'

'Come over here. It stops by those bushes. See? I think we can crawl through them and see what's going on. It's quite easy.'

We pushed through the bushes and there was a whole crowd of people arguing and pushing at one another. The workmen and a crowd of protesters dressed in camouflage green were having a right barney. So we stopped to listen and watch.

'You *can't* build that new road and that thing, whatever it is,' said one of the green men, pointing to the bulldozers, cranes, pipes, wires, concrete, etc, all part of Max's half-built new ride. 'You're destroying the landscape! Some of these trees have been here for over a thousand years.'

'Well, they're not going to be here much longer. This is Mr Moore's land and he can do what he wants on it,' answered a large man, the foreman of the works gang.

'You'll knock them down over our dead

bodies. We're going to occupy these trees. You do realize you'll need planning permission.'

Behind him I caught a glimpse of a figure swinging from one tree to another like Tarzan, landing in a tree house which had just been built.

'We got planning permission. Anyway, look around you. This place is hardly short of trees, is it? What's a few less matter? So get lost,' snapped the foreman.

'I don't believe you, and if you have, then strings have been pulled by someone somewhere,' the green protester said. 'But you'll have to fight us every inch of the way.'

A member of the construction team saw us and came over.

'Sorry, folks, I should move on if I were you. It's a bit dangerous round here at the moment. Go and look at the animals instead.'

'What was all that about?' asked Slug as we walked away. Behind us they were starting to shout.

'Dunno. Someone doesn't want Max to build any more rides,' I said. 'Well, it is his land. He should be allowed to build what he wants on it.'

'Yes, but some of these trees are special. They've been there for yonks,' said Slug.

'Who cares about that?'

'I'd keep the trees,' Marie said.

'I wouldn't. That new thing Max is building looks really . . .' I started, then she finished with 'awesome.'

Marie was strangely silent as she walked ahead back to the castle.

Six

She swept down the wide, curving marble staircase and a huge sigh went up from the crowd in the castle's banqueting hall. Men rushed to the foot of the stairs. Cameras whirred. For Sir Magnus Moore had arrived. He was throwing a party for his special guests to celebrate the première of his new film, and the press and TV people were everywhere, as always when Max turned up anywhere. 'WELCOME' was strung up in flashing lights from beam to beam in the ancient room and music came from a rock group in the corner, the Fried Bangers, Marie said. Flowers, balloons, flashing lights, strobes, flashing jewels . . . wow!

All day people and kids had crowded the park, exploring, guzzling, scaring themselves silly. But they weren't allowed in the castle and the gates had closed at five sharp.

And now night was coming. The party was about to begin! The hall filled up. A huge table at the back was crammed with food and another with drinks. And then *she* appeared, sweeping down the stairs like Cinderella at the ball.

'Isn't she lovely?' shouted someone.

'Isn't she, isn't she?' cried someone else. Cameras clicked, whatnots whirred.

'Lovely, lovely! What a beauty!'

'But who is she?'

'Who is she? She's the most beautiful and heavenly being I've ever seen in all my life,' moaned someone beside me.

Her hair was cropped short, soft and as velvety-black as night, as black as the dress she wore. Her eyes sparkled like stars under thick black eyebrows, her smile was so sweet and gentle it could melt chocolate in a freezer.

'She takes your breath away,' breathed another idiot, while that git Slug murmured, 'Who is she? She must be a princess . . .'

'It's 'er, innit! Sharon,' snapped Marie. 'She's at it again.'

'At what?'

'Oh, don't be so *thick*, Gary. Showing off, of course.'

'Stop saying I'm thick!'

'Mind you, she must have had her teeth fixed. She's had that missing bit of her front one filled.

The one Marshy chipped when they had that row.'

'You got twenty-twenty vision then, Marie?'

'Yep. And I'll tell you something else. She's still wearing her Doc Martens under all that velvet.'

'Great. Then she hasn't really changed,' sighed Slug.

Sharon had paused on the stairs as she was joined by Max, and a cheer went up. He kissed her, then held up his hands for silence so he could speak to the crowd.

'Friends! Dear, dear friends!' he began, when suddenly there was a noisy interruption as a big, hairy bloke burst through the crowd.

'You!' he shouted. 'You're at it again! Why can't you stay the same for five minutes? What have you done to yourself this time, me girl?'

Sharon's face lit up. She grinned – her old wicked grin.

'Dad, you got here!' she bellowed in a voice as loud as his, and jumped down the rest of the stairs, landing on a cameraman's foot. He howled in pain and hobbled away.

'No, she doesn't really change,' cried Marie,

'and that's her own real hair this time.' Then, 'Dad! You came!'

'Dad,' we all yelled and leapt on him, even Slug calling him Dad.

'Helicopter,' he spat out. 'Where's the mad alien pixie?'

'In bed. Where's Mum?'

'She couldn't come.'

'We know. Mrs Birkinshaw wanted her,' we all shouted.

All this time whirring, clicking, lights flashing and shouting was going on, but Max must've got fed up with standing there with his hands held up for quiet, because suddenly there sounded a loud drum roll from the Fried Bangers and then, at last, there was silence.

Max told us how happy he was to see us all for the première of his latest film, a classic Victorian thriller entitled *Barnaby Barnes*, about a murder in a murky London street which was solved with the help of the brave orphan boy Barnaby. This gave him great pleasure because it was on this very same street where the film was made that he had met beautiful Sharon who was now his wife (cheers!). And her family. Here, all the cameras trained on us just as Nanny Drain

Cover and Purdey Perdita appeared with Ems, blinking, sleepy and cross from being woken up.

'Those pictures'll be awful,' I whispered to Marie. 'What with ole Drain Cover, Ems and Slug on 'em.'

'And you . . .' she said, smiling at the cameras.

Then Max took Sharon by the hand and led the crowd down some corridors to his own private theatre, as he called it, tucked away in another part of the castle. It sloped down, big and plush with pop-up seats, and we all sat on the front row, though Dad had disappeared somewhere.

'I don't think he likes Victorian films much,' said Marie.

'He'll have gone for a drink at the bar,' I answered, tucking in to some popcorn I'd got stashed away.

'Shush,' someone said, taking it off me. 'We want to hear the soundtrack.'

I was miffed. Still, at least Ems wasn't there to wreck it. She'd been taken back to bed.

Our street looked dirty and miserable and slummy and scruffy in the film.

'Glad Mum's not here,' Marie muttered.

Still, I liked bits of it. I saw my face twice – I looked OK – and Slug's, looking horrible. Marie floated around as a sort of angel-guardian-spirit. Didn't think much of her. Ems looked like a mad Martian. The bits I really liked were the murderer getting bashed on the head and the fight near the end. When the lights went on Marie was wiping her eyes.

'It was beautiful,' she sniffed. 'Barnaby was so sweet and touching.'

'Was he? You surprise me.'

'Oh, Gary, you're not only thick, you've got no poetry or feeling in you.'

'Hey, that's not fair. I have got feeling – I jumped out of my seat when that kid whatsisname fell off the roof. And my foot's gone to sleep.'

'Shush! Max is going to speak!'

'Oh, not again!'

The crowd stopped leaving to hear Max thank them once more and ask them to look out for his next film, which would be full of new original ideas.

'We don't get many avant-garde films in this country,' he said. 'I want to be in the forefront of some new thinking. Please support me.'

Clapping and cheers, so Marie didn't hear me ask her what the heck he was on about, and really I didn't care as I could hear music and I knew there was grub kicking around in the banqueting hall.

Part Three

One

Now the party was really hopping.

Drink flowed.

Food everywhere.

Music blared out, echoing through the castle on loudspeakers. Groups of grown-ups in fancy dress stood around drinking punch from a huge basin with bits of fruit floating in it. More and more people had changed into fancy dress, and there was Minder Martin in a Gestapo uniform.

'Suits you,' I said. 'Has Nanny Harris got one as well?'

Sharon swanned around in wide skirts and her long blonde wig again.

'Who are you now?' asked Dad, heading for the punch.

'Cinderella!'

'What's Max, then?' we asked.

'He said he was coming as the Invisible Man, so I don't think we'll see him!'

Dad groaned. 'I knew I shouldn't have come!'

'Aren't you pleased to see us, then?'

'Yeah, course I am. But I didn't get dressed up. Didn't have time coming off the oil rig.' He took a large swig of punch.

A figure in a leopard-skin costume came up to him. 'You've come as the working man, I see,' he said.

'I *am* a working man,' said Dad and turned to walk away, followed by Leopard Skin.

I kept sneaking the punch as well, 'cos it was very yummy. Mind you, it did make my head spin quite a bit, but I knew I could handle it. Grown-ups eat, drink and talk an awful lot of rubbish, but if you watch what you're doing you can get by.

'Not too much of that, Gary,' Dad said. 'You're too young.'

'I wish I was in fancy dress,' Marie smiled hopefully at Sharon.

'There's a whole lot of actor's props at the back of that theatre – take a look.'

'Come on, Gary.'

'No way. I'll stay as I am. Like Dad.'

Marie and Slug shot off and I had another swig of punch. Sharon shoved off with a crowd of men round her.

You could hardly move now in the hall, and

the Muzak was blaring out full blast as Marie came back as a lion and Slug as a bear.

'You look like a hyena,' I said to Slug.

They hopped about a bit. Dad returned, looking fed-up.

'You all right, Dad?' asked Marie.

'Yeah,' he said. 'You kids go and enjoy yourselves.'

'Let's get away from here,' I said.

We found a deserted room and played Cowboys and Indians, Hide and Seek, Blind Man's Buff, Pirates, and danced to the music blaring round the castle.

'It's a good job there's no neighbours,' Slug said.

You could have heard the racket miles away. At last we all flopped down on the floor for a rest. But with Marie, tiredness lasted all of five seconds.

'I'm going back to the main party,' she announced. 'You lot coming?'

Slug, her faithful bear, got up and followed her, staggering a bit 'cos he was tipsy too. But I lay there in the empty room, feeling completely knackered. The snake and swamp nightmare had come back last night and Slug had snored, so the punch I'd been swigging was getting to me. I wanted to lie down and snooze, but I was too close to the music. I'd go up to our room at the top of the castle, quieter there, and I could crash out and come down later on.

So I staggered along the corridor, head spinning like a roundabout, and up the stone spiral stairs, looking forward to being there without Slug for once. I'd just reached the top floor when – Shock! Horror! I shook my head and shut and opened my eyes. The punch! Didn't they say drunkards see pink elephants or tropical insects? I shook my head to clear it, but it wasn't pink elephants or tropical insects. It was Ems crawling along the battlements, and there was a hundred-foot drop on the other side down into the moat. She was gurgling happily to herself.

Fear cleared my head like a cloth cleaning a window. What the heck was she doing up here? She must have been put to bed away from the noise. They said she was tucked up in her cot. Trouble was, Ems was like Marie and never stayed tired for long, so she must've woken up, got out of the cot, opened the door and climbed out here.

I lurched forward and grabbed her, pulling away from the drop, and we both banged on the hard stone floor. She pulled my hair, howling, tearing out clumps. But I hardly felt it.

'Oh, Ems, Ems, you're like a cat with nine lives. Except you're using them up too quickly,' I gasped, gazing over the side of the castle. People were now throwing off their clothes and jumping off the drawbridge into the moat, laughing and shrieking with the cold and swimming about, looking fat, bare and awful. The shock of grabbing Ems suddenly mixed with the punch and I did a Slug and threw up over the side. I hope it doesn't land on someone, I thought, but so what? At least I felt a lot better. Then I had a funny feeling someone was watching me – but I'd gone beyond caring.

'C'mon, you,' I said, picking up Ems. I didn't feel tired any more. 'You're coming down to the party. *They* can look after you.'

We returned downstairs to look for the others. I found Marie in the kitchen, helping herself to some snacks.

'You've brought Ems down,' she said.

'Yeah! You can say that again! Is Dad still here?'

'No. Dad's had enough. Says he sick of all the pseuds in this place and if that guy in the leopard costume doesn't leave him alone, he's gonna deck him. So he's phoned for a taxi to take him to the nearest place to here, wherever that is, and find somewhere to stay. He wants to be back with normal people again, he says. This is *not* Dad's scene.'

'P'raps he missed Mum,' I said.

'I phoned up. She couldn't make it. 'Nother crisis,' shrugged Marie.

'So what do we do now? They're getting wild here.'

'Yeah. Let's get back in our games room before we get trampled to death. C'mon.'

Two

We'd only been in the games room a few minutes when a long crocodile of people entered,
arms tangled around each other.

'They're doing the conga,' Marie shrieked.
'C'mon, let's join in.'

So this long chain, growing all the time, went
through the castle, in and out of the rooms, the
corridors and out into the courtyard before
stopping in the hall, where we did the can-can
and the hokey-cokey and back to the conga, legs
going like trees in a hurricane. We rolled on and
on, on and on, me hanging on to Marie and Slug
on to me. Dad was in the line, surprise, surprise,
holding on to a Spanish lady, red frills all over
her and a sort of birdcage on her head.

'This is for wrinklies,' I yelled to Marie.

'Who cares? Retro, innit?'

On and on, head whirling, eyes whizzing,
tired, dizzy, pound, pound, pound to the music
which wasn't gonna stop ever.

Dee dee dee dah CONGA! Dee dee dee dah

CONGA! Was this awful dorky tune that should've died and been buried long ago going to go on for ever and ever and ever and ever and ever? Yeah! No, no, no, no, no.

A figure in black leathers shot in front of Marie and shifted her mitts on to its waist, *dee dee dee dah CONGA*, and took a turn to the left and down, down, down, and then there was only Black Leathers, Marie, Slug and me going *dee dee dee dah CONGA*, just the four of us, down, down, down, down – moving away from the music and party people, but still we couldn't stop, on and on, down and down, *dee dee dee dah CONGA* – Marie going like a tuned-up engine, Slug puffing and blowing like a whale. The corridor turned to a tunnel that narrowed and turned to stone and still we danced on, down, down, down, the walls narrowing and turning – something soft and horrible drifted across my face, deadly fingers reaching out for me to draw me down into the deadly swamp and the snake with its tongue that flickered.

'Marie!' I yelled. 'Stop, stop.'

No one listened. No one stopped. Then we turned another corner and the corridor widened into an empty stone square space in front of an old black door with iron hinges. I'd seen it a thousand times in films and videos and cartoons. The music had faded. We'd stopped at last – Slug slumped, Marie's eyes sparkling.

The figure in black turned round. And it was Sharon, of course – crop-headed Sharon in leathers and boots.

'Listen, you lot . . . You're the only ones I can trust – even if you *are* like something the cat's dragged in.'

'You're up to something, Sharon.' Marie's voice was as soft as cat's fur. 'I know you. What trouble are you lugging us into now?'

Sharon shook her head. She smiled sadly and turned to the door. 'He told me not to come here. I could go anywhere else, but not down here.'

'So, sister Sharon, of course you came here . . .'

'Sure. What else can you do?'

'But if it's forbidden?' Slug croaked.

'Nothing's forbidden to me,' said Sharon. 'He gave me a whole load of keys and cards and I worked out which one this was. Took me ages trying them out. But now here we are. Bluebeard's den.'

'Blue Stubble, you mean,' I said.

'That's a good name for him. You've sussed

him out, have you? Now here goes. I'll open this precious door with this card. I think it's the one.'

'Sharon . . . Sharon – before you do . . .'

'Yes, Slug. What is it?'

'D'you love him?'

'What sort of a question is that? Let's just see what's inside this room he keeps so secret.'

She turned to slide the card into the lock. It *was* the right one, and the door swung open. And then we heard footsteps coming down the echoey stone steps.

'Inside, quick, and I'll shut the door!'

Three

We shot behind the door, cramped together like sardines in an overcrowded can. Slug was trembling so much he'd've fallen over if we hadn't squashed together, holding him up. I didn't feel too good, either. Footsteps stopped at the door.

'Thought it was kept locked,' we could hear a man muttering to himself. Then he came into the room.

This was worse than the swamp and the snake nightmare. Somehow while that was going on, I knew at the back of my mind that I could always wake up out of it if it got really bad. But this – this was for real.

There I was wedged between Sharon (smelling of leather), Marie (smelling of mints) and Slug (smelling of Slug – horrible), waiting for Blue Stubble, me brother, to turn round and see us there, just where we weren't supposed to be, though he must've known that if he told Sharon not to do something she'd do it. She'd have to.

Yuman nature, innit? Teachers and grown-ups ought to know this and then there'd be less aggro everywhere.

Footsteps was taking ages getting through the door – or else time had stopped, waiting, waiting for Maxi. He might only be little, but he was menacing, more scary than Minder Martin, Dennis, Drain Cover, Leopard Skin, our Headteacher and the Ofsted Inspectors who came last term, put together.

But it wasn't him. This wasn't a little guy. *Footsteps* was a great big bloke I hadn't seen before, with a beard – wide and ugly, big-booted and hands like meat joints in the supermarket, reaching out for tapes piled up on shelves. The room was full of computers, filing cabinets, CD racks, videos, speakers – you name it, you'd find it somewhere in that room.

He sorted through the tapes, shaking his head. It took him ages, but at last he found the one he was looking for and fitted it into one of the machines. Then, without turning round – he'd've seen us if he had – he pulled out a chair and sat in front of the screen, a big one which we could see as well. Some scrubby bits flashed on, then he fastforwarded till he got to where he wanted. The film was speckly and streaky, home-made, I think, a bit like the ones Dad fiddles about with.

Slug was wobbling like a jelly and then my nose started to itch and tickle inside. I hadn't got room to scratch it. I was going crazy. I'd have to sneeze – I just must sneeze. No. Hold on. Sharon had her hand over Slug's mouth. I held my breath till I thought I'd burst.

A picture of a beautiful girl smiling flashed up, and then Beardy himself appeared. He made a smirky noise. He was pleased! You could tell by the back of his head. He wanted to watch himself, yuck. The beautiful girl smiled and danced in some draperies. Oh, no, one of those boring films . . . And then another shot! A girl lying flopped out on a stone floor, red hair all over the place. Not the same one, then. The dancing drapery one was a long-haired blonde. Big beastly Beardy looked very pleased with this. There was another flash of him smiling and his back looked smiley as well as he sat watching in that chair. Then something was going on with chains, and though a bit of torture doesn't worry me, Sharon was angry. I could feel her stiff as a poker. Steam was almost coming out of her ears.

Silently as an Indian in the woods, she moved forward and picked up a lampstand off a table near us. One of those iron ones. Then she slammed it on Beardy's head. He fell forward and hit his head on one of the filing cabinets.

There he lay flat out on the floor, bleeding a bit, and all the while his face grinned at us on the screen. Sharon switched it off. She was white as a sheet and black as thunder at the same time.

We came out from behind the door. Marie's face flamed. Slug's was green.

'You've killed him!'

'I hope he's dead,' Sharon snarled.

Marie knelt beside the body, the upturned chair.

'But what are we gonna do? I wish you didn't always lose your cool, Sharon. It always ends up a mess. So, what do we do now?'

'Run,' I put in.

And Slug did what he always does. He was sick all over Beardy's boots.

Four

'Run!' cried Sharon.

'Is he dead? Have you killed him?'

'No. But we've got to get out of here before they find us.'

'What did you do that for, Sharon?'

'Made me angry. Come on. Let's go.'

'What'll happen to us?'

'Nothing if we keep quiet.'

But Marie was still bending over the man.

'We have to get help for him. He *might* die.'

'No way,' snapped Sharon. 'Come on, don't hang about!'

'What about that sick?' I asked.

'Oh, shut up, Gary. Just move – we'll go back to the party and no one will know. He didn't see us. And neither did anyone else. So come on.'

'I don't think we should leave him,' Marie went on.

'I want to go home. I don't feel very well,' Slug whimpered.

'Stop whingeing. Don't waste any more time. Oh, no!'

Footsteps. Again. Coming near. Someone whistling. Quickly and quietly Marie closed the door. Sharon pushed us over to the other side of the room.

'Through that door,' she hissed, for there was another one between the filing cabinets. It wasn't locked. She pushed it open and we'd gone through it before we heard the whistler entering the first room.

'Stop panting, Slug. Shut up!'

'Oh, wow!'

'Lordy, lordy, look at that!'

'FanTASTIC!'

One whole wall of this room was glass, lit up by blue and silver lighting.

Even as we looked a gynormous fish, eyes popping, swam towards us. It wasn't a pretty sight. Worse than the snake, really.

'It's an aquarium!'

'No, Gary! It's the *moat*!'

'Shush! Listen!'

There was more than one person next door – exclaiming, shouting.

'Use the mobile. Get help quickly!'

'It's horrible.'

'He must have felt sick and fallen and banged his head – he was eating and drinking a lot when I saw him last.'

'So was everybody else. I wish they'd hurry up and get here.'

'Well, we mustn't move him till they come.'

'It's funny. He's got bumps front and back. And he threw up on the *back* of his boots though he's lying on his front.'

'Oh, don't worry about that. No one comes down here except us and the Boss. He must've been messing about.'

'Funny, though, he seems to have been watching a video. But it's switched off.'

Slug moaned feebly. Marie put an arm round him and a finger on his lips, yuck.

'Oh, they're coming with a stretcher. Just let's get him upstairs. Come on. Glad you've arrived. Here.'

We played statues as the noises grew louder then died away.

'Right,' said Sharon.

'Let's go,' said Marie.

'Now *remember*. We go back, join the party and we know *nothing* about this at all! Got it clear, Slug, Gary? We don't know *anything*.'

'I wanna go home,' sniffed Slug. 'I want your mum, Gary.'

'Me too.'

'We'll phone her. I promise,' Marie said.

Sharon shut the door.

'I'm glad they found him,' Marie said.

'I couldn't care less,' answered Sharon. 'We've got to get away from here.'

Back we scurried up the stone steps, following her.

'If anyone says anything to us, we got lost dancing. OK?'

Party noises were still all around when we reached the top.

'Now listen. I'm going to join the wrinklies,' murmured Sharon. 'You go to the games room and we don't say anything if we see each other. Wait for me to contact you, understand?'

'OK. Understood.'

We tried to find Dad but all they said was he'd gone back to his oil rig. Then we tried phoning Mum but no one answered at home nor at Mrs Birkinshaw's.

At last we tottered into the games room and collapsed. By then I didn't care about anything, bodies, snakes, swamps, ugly big men with footsteps. What ... did ... they ... matter? They could all do what they liked. Night ... night.

Five

Slug zuzzed in rhythm, a swarm of bees on a summer day.

I shook him. He half-opened one eye.

'Go a-*way*,' he moaned. 'Lemme alone.'

We were in the games room where we'd fallen asleep. Everyone else had gone except for Slug, who looked and sounded worse than usual, still wearing his bear outfit. He opened his other eye, turned over to sleep again, and a gentle throb hit the air. Slug was gearing up once more.

So I lurched over to the door and peered down the corridor, looking around. The whole place looked like a bomb had hit it, a right mess. I could hear Drain Cover telling a group of helpers to clear up the place. No way was I gonna join in, so I went the other way, past Max's study door, which was slightly open for once. I could hear him inside pacing up and down, talking to someone on his mobile. His voice carried over quite clearly.

'You've got rid of those protesters? Good!

They were starting to be a nuisance. Now, I want you and your men to get cracking on that new ride, pronto. This has put us behind schedule. And I have to go away for a few days, so –'

He listened for a moment, then starting talking again.

'No, I don't know why that lot turned up when they did. Someone must've put them up to it. I realize it means that your men will have to do plenty of overtime, but there'll be a bonus in it for you. And with regards to our film project, we'd better get a move on. We need to get it going. Time is of the essence.'

'Time is of the essence,' I mouthed, pulling faces. 'Time is of the essence. Time is –'

'What are you muttering about?' Max stood there in front of me. Not much bigger than me, but full of menace.

'Sir! Sorry, Sir!'

'Go on. Go and enjoy yourself with the others.'

I ran down the corridor to the kitchen and looked round the door. Marie was there, busy feeding Ems, both looking as bright-eyed and bushy-tailed as ever in their ordinary clothes. Last night didn't seem to have had any effect on them.

'Hi, Gary. You're up at last,' she said. 'Where's David?'

'He's still asleep, and from the look of him I don't think he's gonna get up today.'

'Lazybones. Want anything to eat?'

She was stuffing down bacon, sausages, eggs, muffins, waffles, fried potatoes and beans. I joined in and whispered to her about Max's phone call. Her eyes flashed.

'Let's go and take a look – see what's going on out there.'

'I dunno. They might make us clear off again.'

'No, they won't. That was 'cos those other people were there. Besides, there's nuffin to do round here unless you want to help tidy up. And anyway, I want to talk to you.'

'What about?'

'You know what about.'

'OK, then.'

'Shall we get David? He might want to come.'

'You're joking,' I said.

We went to the games room. He was still flat out.

'We're going out, Slug. D'ya wanna come?'

'Ooooh! Oooh! Oh! No!'

'You sure 'bout that?'

'No, no, no!'

I put Ems beside him. She pulled his hair and tweaked his ear, making him groan even louder.

'Well, if you don't wanna come, there's some lovely grub for breakfast. Lashings of streaky bacon and lovely runny fried eggs . . .' I licked my lips, making slurping sounds.

'Gary, stop it. You're making him sick . . .'

'So what? He makes me feel sick.'

Slug had turned green.

'LEAVE ME ALONE!' he bellowed. 'Let me die in peace!'

'Let's go, Gary,' said Marie. 'He's not feeling very well.'

As we walked over to the drawbridge, Pretty Girl Purdey came and collected Ems and took her off in her buggy. I looked back hopefully at the cars parked in the courtyard.

'No chance of a lift from anyone, I s'pose.'

'Gary! What do you think you've been given legs for? Let's walk. It's good for you.'

'Great. That's really good to know.'

'Besides, I want to talk to you.'

'What about?'

'You know. Last night.'

'I want to forget about it. It's like my old nightmares and I always try to forget them.

Why can't we talk about this some other time?'

'*No*! I want to do it *now*! So come on.'

I stopped trying to argue. Once Marie had decided she wanted to do something, that was it. So we walked down the road looking at the animals, who all seemed a bit hungover like Slug. Perhaps all that music blaring out had taken its toll on them too. Marie said she wanted to talk, but all she came up with was, 'There's something going on here, Gary.'

'I know. But I've got blisters and that's all I care about now.'

'Just come on.'

With my aching legs and foot blisters we reached the theme park area, deserted except for the group of workmen busy on the new ride, still a mass of concrete, metal and wires at the moment. There was no sign of the tree protesters, like the man had said. Even the one who'd swung through the trees had gone. Or had he? He wasn't in a tree any more, but as I gazed around I was sure that there was a figure wearing a green camouflage jacket watching the men from a bush.

'Look!'

'Yes, I've seen him too,' Marie said.

'Why's he stayed behind when the others have gone?' I asked.

'Dunno. Let's go and ask him and find out.'

So we headed towards the bush, but by the time we got there he was gone as well.

'Weirder and weirder.'

'Gary, let's go and look at that notice.'

We were now on a little hill looking down on the park and we could see a couple of workmen banging a large notice into the ground. We approached warily, not wanting to annoy the men, and took a look. In black letters over a red and yellow flame background it said:

GO ON THE RIDE TO ARMAGEDDON IF YOU DARE.

YOU WILL RIDE UP TO THE HEAVENS AND DOWN TO THE DEPTHS

AND EXPERIENCE SOMETHING THE LIKES OF WHICH

NO MERE MORTAL HAS EVER WITNESSED BEFORE.

I read it and whistled.

'Cor, that sounds pretty awesome. Can't wait to have a go.'

'Me, too,' said Marie. 'Let's try and have the *first* go, shall we?'

'We'd better be gettin' back,' I said. 'We've got to wait for Sharon to contact us.'

All that day we waited. But we never saw her at all.

And nobody, nobody mentioned the body in the dungeon room.

Six

The rain fell straight as rulers down into the moat – splish, splash, splish, splash – as we watched it through the pointy window.

'We can't go out in that,' I said happily.

'No. Well, if we're staying indoors I'd like to prowl round the library. Hundreds of books there,' Marie replied. 'And I want to find Sharon,' she added, as Drain Cover appeared to dress Ems, who ran shrieking round the room.

'And there are all those collections in the castle – stamps, coins, butterflies . . . I'd love to see them,' cried Slug.

'I just want to watch telly,' I moaned. 'I don't want to go *learning* things, Marie.'

'Why don't you just turn into a couch potato and be done with it?' she snapped. 'You are the laziest person in the world, Gary. You never want to do anything!'

'No, I'm not. And yes, I do. I do want to watch telly.'

'Well, there's a room with an absolutely

gigantic, enormous one next to the library. Come on,' said Marie, then, turning to Drain Cover, 'Is Max around today?' she asked innocently.

'Sir Magnus has gone up to London early. He will be away for a day or two,' she replied, sniffing. 'Not that it's any of your business, children.'

'Where's Sharon, then?' went on Marie.

'Madam will be somewhere in the Castle. In her boudoir trying on clothes. That's what she usually does.' She sniffed even louder and rammed Ems into *her* clothes.

After breakfast me, Marie and Ems went to Sharon's and Max's private rooms while Slug went off on his own. But they were locked so we wandered through the corridors looking for Sharon, no luck.

'Might as well go to the library,' Marie said.

It was a long, long way. After a bit . . . 'I think we're lost . . .'

'I'm always lost here.'

But Pretty Girl Purdey popped round the corner, so we asked her.

'You go straight on past the Roman urns, then left, past the pre-history section, then the gallery of statues, up the flight of stone stairs, then left and past the orchid conservatory, and the museum areas are on the right and the library's next door and then the TV room.'

'Oh! Thanks! You sure we don't have to go round the world as well while we're about it?'

She smiled at me. 'No, Gary. Just keep going and you'll get there eventually. Always remember that. Oh, and sorry – can you keep Ems for now? There's something I must do. And Gary . . . Take care. And look after them.'

Then she was gone.

'What does she mean?' cried Marie. 'It's me that looks after everything and everybody.'

'That's what you think.'

She shut her lips tight, stuck her nose in the air and didn't speak until we reached the library and museum.

'You go on there . . .' She pointed at a door at the end. 'Take Ems with you. I'll join you when I've finished looking at everything and you can look after us all again. Huh, fat chance. I'm off to do something.'

The television was as big as a room. I plonked Ems down in front of it, found the control and switched on. A gun battle in a dark shed leapt out at us. Bangs, blood and bodies all over everywhere, so big we were almost in there with all the action.

'Great,' I said to Ems.

Bang, bang, bang went Blah as well as the guns. Ems grinned all over her funny face. She was happy.

We settled in, Ems and me.

Ages later Slug joined us.

'Wonderful! Brilliant! You should've come with me. Gary, those butterflies are out of this world. Max had got a very rare –'

'Oh, belt up! You're boring. Get a load of this.'

'*That's* boring – just another old gun battle. Get rid of it. Change channels, Gary.'

'No!'

'Oh, please.'

'You've been doing what you want . . .'

'But this is so feeble.'

'Well, no, it's not so brilliant as the first one I watched. Ems has dozed off. She loved the violent siege of Bloodthirsty Ranch.'

'Oh, Gary.'

'Well, try this. Cartoon? That do you?'

'The screen's so *big*,' said Slug. 'I feel as if I'm in with . . .'

'You nearly are ... Look, it's our castle. There!'

Battlements and towers against the sky, a moat, drawbridge, portcullis, courtyard, views of long corridors, steps, stairs, statues – then a girl, a pretty girl, long blonde hair like Sharon's on the day of the party, creeping secretly along a dark corridor, going down steps leading into even darker stone passages till, coming to a little door set deep in the wall, she stopped, looked at the heavy key-ring in her hand, then put one into the lock in the door, turned it and went into a dungeon ...

Slug screamed. 'I don't like this place,' he moaned.

The sound rang through the room. Ems woke up and buried her face in Blah. In the dungeon five heads were hanging on hooks tied up by their long blonde hair, while Slug kept babbling on about it only being a cartoon.

And as we sat staring Marie shot in.

'Come and look, you lot – there's something I want to show you.'

We ran after her past the Roman urns and the statues, then turned left past more doors and chairs and pots standing on shelves and tables and then a long row of portraits on the walls. At last we arrived in front of a door painted black instead of white.

'Shush . . .' she said. We tiptoed after her into a big square room with dark walls and white velvet curtains. The walls were hung with dozens of photographs on two sides and paintings on the other two. In the centre of the room was a platform on which stood five painted statues, horribly lifelike.

Slug was shivering. 'I don't like it here. It's spooky!'

Marie was stroking the statues – I told you she was brave. I wouldn't have touched them with Ems's buggy.

'They all look the same,' I said. 'Crazy! Why all the same?'

'They're waxworks,' Marie put in softly. 'Like in Madame Tussaud's. Went there on a school trip last year.'

'It's like a tomb – a graveyard,' whispered Slug.

'But they're not all the same,' Marie went on, investigating everything, yuck. 'They're different . . . yet . . .'

Ems stirred in her buggy as footsteps sounded.

'Someone's coming. Let's get out of here. They're round that corner. Go the other way. Fast.'

We sped down the corridor like players in a computer game. Safely back outside again, we took a breath in the courtyard while Ems struggled out of her buggy.

'Why did we run away?' Marie asked. 'No one told us not to go in there. I thought it was locked when I saw it first. But the key was in the door.'

'So what?' I said.

She pulled a face at me. 'I only wanted a look, didn't I? And I tell you something. Those girls in there all look a bit like Sharon.'

'Must be his type,' I said.

'Sharon's anybody's type,' sighed Slug. 'She's beautiful.'

Seven

Marie dragged us for miles. Away from the castle, the restaurant, the novelty shops, past the maze, the craft shops, the Ancient Barn, the water-falls, the railway line running along by the lake, bypassing the deer park, the monkey house, the zebras, the elephants, the rhinos, the lion enclosure and the tiger enclosure with its tigers, two of them white. You name it, we passed it, Marie pushing Ems like Boadicea with a buggy instead of a chariot. Ems shrieked now and then, wanting out, but Marie only paused to push a lolly in her mouth and rushed on.

'I've got a stitch,' I wailed. Nobody cared. Slug had turned pink and purple and was puff-ing too much to speak, maybe he'd have a heart attack with all those crisps he eats. On and on we pounded up through the woods on a steep stony path beside the tracks of the Armageddon ride, which was almost ready for opening.

'I shall die,' I groaned. 'Can't we just stop?'

'Not till I'm sure no one's listening!' hissed

Marie. She wasn't even out of breath, just gently pink.

She struck away from the path, deeper into the woods, crash, bang, through the undergrowth, disturbing all the wildlife that wasn't in the enclosures. Marie unfastened Ems, handed me the buggy and hoisted Ems on to her shoulders. We charged on and on.

At last, 'Here!' she commanded. 'This'll do.'

We'd arrived at a mossy hollow under the trees, hidden by bushes with big, glossy leaves. Her eyes were enormous, not soup plates, dinner plates.

'Listen,' she said. 'Listen!'

'We *are* listening. You don't have to say it twice, Marie.'

We waited, mouths open, panting, Ems licking her lolly.

'This is an absolute, utter secret. Don't say anything to *anybody*! Promise?'

'Yeah. Yeah!'

'Repeat after me. Cross your hearts and hope to die!'

'Cross your hearts and hope to die!' Slug muttered faithfully.

'No! You stupid git! You say, "Cross my heart and hope to die." And *you*, Gary.'

'No, I won't. I don't want to die, Marie, so I'm not gonna say I hope to – so shut up and get on with it. And hurry up. I'm bursting.'

'You should've gone before.'

'You didn't give me any time.'

Something dark flew just above us, making me jump in the air. Slug moaned. This place gave me the creeps.

'Oh, blow this!' I exploded, leapt up and ran behind a bush.

Coming back, feeling better, I said. 'Go on. Get on with it.'

Marie looked all around her, then leaned forward and whispered, 'Listen.'

We listened.

She looked round again, then whispered something.

'I can't hear you. Speak up!' I said.

'Sharon. I think she's in danger. Terrible danger. We've got to save her! And maybe we're in danger, too!'

We sat staring at each other.

'What are you on about now, Marie? You gone crazy? Again? Marie, say something. Answer.'

'Gary, what I know is . . .'

'What? Get on with it.'

'Remember the waxworks we saw? I went there again when nobody was about and peeped in and two guys were working on them and I heard one say, "I bet we'll soon be getting another to add to the collection. His latest. I think he prefers waxworks to the real thing . . ." '

'What's he mean by that?' Slug asked.

'He's only gonna have another one made like Sharon, stoopid,' I snapped.

'I wasn't sure,' said Marie slowly, 'so I waited for them to leave and then – I crept up to look at them more closely – and, and . . .' She shuddered.

'Go on.'

'I saw a – *bone* – sticking out of a big toe. Then I ran away.' She hid her face.

Slug started to cry. Ems banged him with Blah.

'Don't talk crap, Marie. People can't do things like that these days. It's not much to go on, is it? Two blokes 'aving a natter. And a big toe that probably wasn't a real big toe. We're more likely to get into trouble over going down in *that* place and Sharon bashing that man.'

'People *do* get murdered. You don't read the papers like I do. They're *full* of people getting done in and Horrible Happenings! I know something's going on here! Dungeons, films and now statues!'

'Belt up, Slug. Crying won't help.'

'Gary, remember that reporter, Polly Sims?'

'Was that 'er name?'

'Yeah. Well, she's still missing. And she was investigating and writing about him. I think she found out something and got murdered. And got pushed in the moat!'

'I know, let's run away,' sniffled Slug.

'What? Stuck out here miles from anywhere?'

'Oh, oh,' wailed Slug. 'I wish we'd never come. I wish Sharon had stayed off that man.'

'Anyway, we can't leave Sharon on her own in danger,' said Marie. 'We must save her.'

'What? Us? We're not into saving people. Look at us. Slug's useless and Ems is in a buggy. That leaves you and me. And I'm not into saving people, like I said.'

'We've got to be brave and clever!' Marie hissed.

'That lets me out.'

'Don't be a wimp, Gary. We're gonna take another look at those waxworks – then find out what happened to the other wives. And we're gonna find Sharon. Then tell the police.'

'Us and who else? The angels? You're barmy.

Get a life in this world, Marie. I don't want your alternative adventures. I'm sure it's all a loada rubbish and you can get stuffed! Ouch!' I yelled as Ems hit me very hard with Blah.

'Gary!'

'Yes, Marie. OK, OK, OK. Maybe, maybe. I'll help, anyway.'

Eight

'Oh, there you are,' cried a voice, one of our favourites. 'I've been searching for you wee bibbies everywhere. The castle's all cleaned up now and so you can go for a walk and git some frish air in your lungs after lunch. I'm busy so you can go to the adventure park till it's time for your supper. And a wee word now. Don't go nosing around all over the place. You're very privileged children being invited here, so just see that you behave yourselves and don't stick your noses in where you shouldn't.'

She walked away. Marie stuck out her tongue after her.

'I want to look round some more.'

'Do you think we should, Marie?' I asked. ''Cos she scares me silly, she's like a dog worrying a bone. She just won't let go.'

'Come on,' she ordered.

'Where are we going?' I asked as we hurried after her.

'To that big barn-like place in front of that

field behind the maze. The one with the big double doors.'

'Oh, I don't want to go all that way! What use is it gonna be?'

'Shut up. I want to see what's in there.'

'It'll be locked. We shan't be able to get in.'

It was. Padlocked. I was glad.

'Can we go and get something to eat now, Marie? I'm starving.'

Slug had been carrying Ems piggy-back and now put her down wearily. She shot forward on her podgy legs towards a small bush with flowers on it. She went to pick one – then suddenly crouched down and wriggled into a little gap underneath the building before we could catch her. We tried to follow, but the gap was too small for us.

'Ems,' we called. 'Ems. Come back!'

She was chuckling madly. Awful sounds. Smashing things with a hammer or something. Ems was letting rip in there – we had to stop her. . . A sound of glass breaking reached our ears, a well-known sound. Ems sometimes wrecked things at home but there was usually someone to stop her before she did too much damage. But here we couldn't stop her. We wrenched frantically at the door to no avail. I put my eye to a knothole and looked through it to see a helicopter with Ems sitting in it holding a brick and gurgling happily. How in crazy did she get in? But Ems could always get in anywhere.

'Ems, come out,' I begged.

'Ems. Ems,' hissed Marie. 'If you don't come, I'll give Blah to the lion.'

We heard a squeak and soon she wriggled back to us the way she had come.

'Oh, crumbs. I hope Max doesn't want to use his helicopter for a few days. She's smashed the windscreen. Must've climbed up that stepladder.'

'Oh, Ems, you wicked creature,' cried Marie. 'If anyone asks, we don't know anything, OK, Gary?'

'Why should we own up? We didn't do anything and Ems is too young to know better.'

'Let's get away from here, then, or someone might guess we did it and tell him.'

'I wouldn't like to be that person,' said Slug. 'It seems we're not telling about a lot of things.'

'And there's a lot of things they're not telling us,' Marie snapped.

On the way back to the castle Marie kept on

about how important it was to find Sharon and phone Mum and Dad. Then she started off again about the reporter Polly Sims who went missing. Like I told you, she never lets go of anything once she's got her teeth into it and, thinking of teeth, I said, partly to shut her up, 'P'raps your lion ate her.'

'Don't be silly. Anyway, I want to go and see him again.'

I wished I'd never mentioned him.

'What do you want to see that mangy old beast again for?'

'He's not mangy, he's lovely.'

'Well, I'm not walking miles again. I'm only going if the train's running today.'

'I'm going whether the train is running or not. So is David.'

'Sure am,' said Slug.

He'd go and jump off a cliff if she asked him to, I thought.

The railway was open. Marie was quiet as we rode along. Finally she said, 'I don't trust Max, y'know.'

'He likes you,' said Slug. 'I heard him say so.'

'Well, I just don't like him. He's a monster.'

'I've just seen your lion,' I said, hoping to change the subject in case anyone heard her.

And it might cheer her up. But she still seemed down and cross.

So did Joe the lion when we got off the train and went to see him. He was back in the lion enclosure and he didn't seem happy with the other lions, who were all in a group together, leaving him all alone. He was trying to chew something which looked like an old bone and finding it difficult with his dental problems. Then he looked up, saw Marie, perked up and came over to the fence. She tried to stroke his tatty mane, but couldn't reach him through the double wire. She put down Ems, who was squealing, and then she and the lion stood looking at each other like parted lovers. Amazing.

'I wish I could let him out,' she said. 'He doesn't like being in there.'

Me, I was glad he was in there even if he had no teeth or claws to speak of. He was still dangerous-looking enough. Cunningly, I suggested, 'What about the other lions? If you let him out they'd all escape too.'

'It's not a good idea, Marie,' said Slug, for once.

'Maybe you're right,' she said.

I looked up and saw a huge figure approaching.

'Dennis is coming,' I said. We turned away and Joe went back to his bone-like thing. I couldn't make out what it was.

'Shall we go over to the park?' asked Slug.

'No, I'm not in the mood,' said Marie. 'Might as well go back and see if we can find Sharon. She must be somewhere. Oh, Gary, maybe she's gone missing like Polly Sims.'

'Shut up!' I shouted. 'I don't want to listen to you.'

She pulled a face as we were crossing the bridge over the lake.

'There's a crocodile,' cried Slug.

'Want occy,' shouted Ems, reaching over to it.

'No!' screamed Marie. 'Occy will have you if you're not careful.'

'Having problems?' smiled Pretty Purdey, suddenly there out of nowhere and giving Ems a bar of chocolate which shut her up.

'What about me?' I asked.

'You're sweet enough, Gary,' she laughed, and hurried away.

We wandered on, exploring, sussing out the place, for Marie said we had to as it was so huge. I just went along wiv 'er.

Then I saw him.

'Look, look. He's there. That green man. I caught sight of him just there!'

'Where?' asked Slug.

'Over there, pinhead. Among those trees! *Look!*'

Woods surrounded the sides and the back of the castle and it was there I'd seen him.

'There's no one there. You're imagining things, Gary.'

'You said I hadn't any imagination. But he's gone now. I can't see him any more.'

'*If* he is here, he's up to somethin',' Marie said. 'Let's try and catch him and find out.' Her eyes shone. Adventure time? 'We can split up, then we've got more chance of catching him.'

I wasn't very keen on this idea at all.

'What if he doesn't want to be caught?' I protested. 'He might be dang'rous!'

'You're just a scaredy-cat,' said Marie.

'Well, I'm not lookin' for him on my own. All together or nuffin.'

'I know,' she said. 'You and David go one way, me and Ems the other. Just yell or run away if he gets nasty.'

'Triffic,' I said as she walked away, carrying Ems.

'She's so brave,' said Slug admiringly.

'Loony, you mean,' I muttered as we entered the wood, squeezing through the undergrowth and climbing over fallen branches. We couldn't see him now we were among the trees, and I hoped that we didn't find him. Nervous and ready to run anytime, I peered ahead. And tripped over something.

'Slug! Slug! There! See! I told you!'

Almost hidden behind a bush was a pile of wood, branches and leaves, with a bit of green canvas poking through.

'This must be his den,' I whispered.

'Yeah. Maybe.'

'Maybe! Maybe! What's maybe? *Look!* Over there! You can see him now. Even if you are blind as a bat and thick as planks.'

'Isn't that Marie?'

'No, of course it's not. Does it look like Marie?'

A rustling sound – and a camouflaged figure with dusty dreadlocks and a rucksack on his back emerged for a minute. Gobsmacked, we all stared at one another. Then he turned and skedaddled at ninety m.p.h. or k.p.h. or whatever.

'Marshy, it was Marshy. Gary, it was Marshy. I saw him.'

133

'I know it was Marshy, idiot. C'mon, let's catch 'im. Run!'

We ran and ran after him, but it was no good. He was faster than us and had completely vanished into the woods.

Later Marie and Ems caught up with us. But when we told Marie she didn't seem very excited or even interested.

'You're jealous!' I told her, but she just shrugged.

That night I had a nightmare again and woke up at three o'clock in the morning sweating like mad, heart pounding wildly. Then the drone of Slug's snoring slowly brought me back to earth. I was safe, if fed up with him.

But this dream was different from my snake one. It was very lifelike and in it I was sure that what the lion had been eating was in fact a human foot.

Part Four

One

A huge banner was being hung over the castle wall announcing, 'Welcome'.

'Fat welcome,' I muttered. 'Who for?'

By the portcullis was pinned a notice:

The Magnus Moore Estate is having a special day for the public with all tickets half-price and children under 14 free!!! Take advantage of this wonderful offer and come and marvel at the medieval castle with its rich ancient heritage, travel on the railway through the wildlife park with its wide variety of exotic species and then enjoy the thrills and spills of the theme park with the most up-to-the-minute, brand new, innovative and exciting rides to suit all ages and tastes. Have a great day out!

As we were reading it a procession of cars drew up. Max stepped out of the long black limo. Roaring behind rode a crowd of photographers.

'Hey! Where's your lovely wife? Give us a

break! Let's see some action! Get snogging! Dig her out. Are you expecting a little Moore yet? Hey! Hey!'

We ran off as fast as possible.

That morning Nanny Drain Cover had got up early, leaving us to look after ourselves. Great.

In the castle everywhere had gone crazy for some grand opening. The place was a madhouse, with Nanny Drain Cover organizing the hoovering, dusting, sweeping, polishing, arranging, moving furniture about. They didn't even let us finish our breakfast.

We tried to ring Mum and Dad, but there was no answer and we got hustled on.

'Get out the way,' everybody said. 'We want to clean here.'

'What are we gonna do?' I asked as we wandered off.

'Dunno. I wish we could find Sharon somehow,' said Marie, 'and then get away together.'

'Let's see if Purdey knows where she is.'

I wanted to see Purdey. She was the nicest thing in the whole place. But we couldn't find her anywhere, either.

'Well, I want some more grub. I'm still hungry,' I said.

'You don't think about anything but your stomach. I'm going to see if I can find Sharon. She must be somewhere.'

'Do you want me to come?' asked Slug.

'Nah. It's OK. You two look after Ems.'

So we headed back for the kitchen as Marie disappeared.

We were just getting stuck in when Marie suddenly rushed back in and grabbed my arm.

'Gary, come quick,' she said.

'Urrgghhh!' I spluttered through a mouthful of bread. 'What is it? Let me finish.'

'Come on, it's important.' She kept tugging me.

'I'll come with you if you want,' said Slug.

'Thanks, David,' she said, 'but it's somethin' I want Gary to see. Can you look after Ems for a sec?'

'Sure,' he said, helping himself to some toast. I wanted to stay and have some more, but Marie can never take no for an answer.

'What is it?' I asked irritably. 'Can't it wait?'

'No, it can't,' she said, hauling me along to the bottom of the stairs, which we started to climb. 'I was going along to the library to see if she was in there, though it's not likely, being Sharon, when

I saw the door to a room marked PRIVATE was slightly open and there was a light on.'

'Did you go in?'

'No, I went and got you. I wanted someone else to see it too.' We were now in the corridor outside the room.

'Look, the light's still on. It's still open,' she said.

I suddenly felt worried. 'Marie, be careful,' I said. 'If it's private we might not be s'posed to go in there.'

'We'll just peek round the door and if anyone's in there we'll just forget about it, OK?'

'All right. You look first. I'll keep watch here.'

So I looked down the corridor and she looked in the room.

'Gary, there's nobody there. And no one about. Let's go in.'

We entered, though I didn't want to. Marie wasn't nervous, but I sure was. I felt that we shouldn't be in there and I didn't want to get caught. I wanted to run away.

But Marie would call me chicken. It was a square-shaped panelled room crammed with more videos and cameras and other gear – this place was stuffed to the top towers with technology. There was a door leading into another little room. It looked a bit like an office, really.

'Right, we've seen it,' I said. 'Let's go before someone comes.' Marie had picked up one of the video boxes and was looking at it closely. 'Gary, take a look at this.'

'What about it? Max makes films. We know that,' I said.

'Gary, *look* at it. It's horrible!'

The cover of the box was marked XXX-rated and had a picture of someone in chains being tortured – a video nasty like Big Ugly Beardy was watching. Marie picked up some more.

'Gary, what does it mean? I didn't know he made films like this.'

'Nor me. Marie, let's get out of here! Quick!'

But she'd already gone into the little room leading off this one. I wanted to run, but I couldn't leave her there. Didn't she ever get scared?

'Come in here! Look!'

Oh, no. Don't make me go in there.

'Come on. Quick!'

So I went in. The room was a photographer's darkroom with pictures being developed. Marie picked up a couple and showed them to me.

'Look who's on this one.'

'It's Sharon. No, it's not. But it's someone just like her.'

Marie whispered, 'Oh no! And here. Look at this!'

It looked like a dungeon with two men in it I'd seen before.

'I know who they are. That's the one Sharon bashed on the head and he's the one who was dressed as a leopard at the party. The one Dad didn't like.'

'There's more of them as well, with some other people,' she said. 'Oh, how horrible. That girl's a prisoner. Do you think it's Polly Sims?'

'I dunno. I dunno anythin'. Look, we've got to get out of here! If they know we've found these . . . Let's shut the door and put the videos back and pretend we've never been in here.'

'Gary, we've got to get the police.'

'Yeah, I know. But we've got to get away from here first. NOW!'

Two

We collected Slug and Ems and, desperate, we again began to look for Sharon one more time. But we didn't want to run into Max and his hangers-on so we started to search the grounds – talk about needles in haystacks – miles and miles and miles of theme parks, adventure parks and woods, to say nothing of wild animals. And we'd got Ems with us, showing us up, though she was quiet for once. Tears were running silently down Slug's orangey-grey cheeks.

'Wot's the matter wiv you?' I snapped.

'I wanna be back in our street doing ordinary things. I'm scared all the time here.'

Marie patted him. 'Don't be. It's an adventure, innit?'

'I wish you'd keep your rotten, lousy, stinkin' toe-rag, flea-bitten adventures to your rotten self,' I couldn't help saying. 'I want no part of 'em. I never wanted to be a hero. I just want the new football season. I don't know *nuffink* about anyfink that matters stuck away in this – this phoney place. Where we going, Marie? Not into all them woods?'

'Maybe we can see Marshy. And tell him about things, at least.'

'I thought you didn't believe me.'

'Well, you thought wrong, Gary. Was it here you spotted him?'

'A bit further on there's summat like a den. That's where he hangs out, I reckon. Come on. Follow me. It's fairly well hidden.'

It was. There were the humped-up ferns and straw and branches hidden behind a bush.

And there, deep in the bit of old canvas I'd spotted earlier, were Marshy and Sharon, fast asleep, arms wrapped tight round each other. What you could see of her looked as scruffy as he did.

'Look, she's got all her earrings back. And her nose-ring,' whispered Marie. 'Come on, let's leave them.'

I nearly exploded, 'Wha'? Ain't we gonna tell them everything?'

'No, they're happy, Gary. There'll be trouble enough for them later. Come on.'

And we turned to go.

She was right. Trouble had arrived already. Four men stepped out of the trees, Minder Martin, Driver Dennis, Leopard Man and Max. It was my worst nightmare of all come true.

Max, who was carrying a gun, said gently, 'Oh dear, oh dear, oh dear. I think it's time for you to wake up, dear wife.'

And time stopped as we looked at one another and waited for Sharon and Marshy to wake up.

They stood up, slowly, slowly.

'Take him away and lock him up,' Max ordered. Marshy looked very little being dragged away between two monstrous men. But as he went, he pulled round to Sharon and called, 'Sorry, sorry. I love you, Sharon.'

Sharon stood there wearing an old shirt of Marshy's and her earrings and as she'd done before, she spat on one of Max's shoes – he was wearing smart ones – then the other.

'I despise you. I told you once to get a real life. You should've done it instead of living out one of your own tenth-rate films.'

'Why did you marry me then, my dear?'

'I quite liked you then. I thought you'd give me a career. But I soon knew the only part you'd got for me was that of another victim, Mr Bluebeard.'

'Speaking of Mr Bluebeard, may I have my keys and cards back, please?'

'I haven't got them.'

'Oh, I think I can see them in the pocket of that disgusting shirt you're wearing. Hand them over.' He waved the gun at her.

Sharon did. He looked at them, then picked out the card she'd used.

'Bent, I see. And what's this? Specks of blood? I always thought it might be you bashing up my sculptor, poor fellow. But he'll be better in time to make some *new* statues.'

'I call you Mr Blue Stubble,' cried Marie, who can never keep quiet for long. 'And what have you done with Polly Sims and the other girls in the videos? And leave Sharon *alone*,' she shouted. 'I've told people about you. You won't get away with things! Murderer!'

'What spirit! What talent! I almost feel like keeping you on for later when I've finished with your dear sister here. But what are the kids of today coming to, Edwin? Poking and nosing into things they shouldn't. Naughty, naughty.'

'Well, I think it's because their parents don't seem bothered about them, but then they aren't very good parents, are they? Haven't taken much care of them at all,' said Edwin, the Leopard Man.

'Leave my family alone. They haven't done anything,' cried Sharon.

'What have you done with those girls?' repeated Marie. 'And where's Polly Sims?'

Max flashed his Cheshire Cat smile. He didn't seem in the least bothered that we had found him out. This worried me.

'I'll give you a clue, shall I? Well, as you know, among my many activities I run a wildlife park. And the animals, well, they get hungry . . .'

'So that *was* a foot that old lion was chewing,' I blurted out, managing to speak at last. Slug whimpered. Marie looked at me in surprise.

'Oh, you noticed, did you? Thanks for reminding me. I'd better get Dennis to clear out the cages. Wouldn't do to let our visitors tomorrow see bits of foot lying around in cages, would it?'

'Are you sure you ought to tell them these things?' asked the Leopard Man.

'Why not? They're not going to be able to tell anyone about it.'

'You horrible man!' Marie shouted. 'Why are you doing all these evil things?'

'The usual reasons. Money, for one. You don't think I made my fortune making old period dramas about castles, do you? These other films make far more money. And besides, I enjoy making them. So does Edwin.'

The Leopard Man shrugged his shoulders, giving me the shivs. What was he thinking? I didn't like to guess.

'You won't get away with this,' said Marie. 'If you kill us, our mum and dad'll come looking for us. They *are* good parents. They love us. You've got it wrong.'

Max laughed at the idea. Didn't anything bother him, I wondered?

'Theme parks and wildlife parks and castles are dangerous places, my dear. Accidents can and do happen. You could drown in the lake, in a boating accident, get eaten by wild animals, or crash on one of the fairground rides. That's what happens to people who nose into my business. You could be buried under the foundations of my new Armageddon ride, for instance. I'm sure I can think of a nice juicy ending for you lot. And the film of that will make a lovely lot of money.'

'What about the police, then?'

'They won't find anything. I'm clearing out all the videos in here to sell over the next few days. And they won't find you, or your videos, I promise.'

As he talked, I thought about trying to run for it before they could catch me. Marie stood tense beside me and I guessed she had the same idea. But Max's gun was pointed at Sharon, and his horrible friend was blocking my way, so how? And then Minder Martin returned, together with Dennis.

'You've settled him, then? Good. Well,' smiled Max, 'I've got another little job for you. I want all this lot locked away safely.'

Just then, Ems, who'd dropped off to sleep, awoke and wailed. Minder Martin moved towards her.

'Oh, no,' bawled Marie. 'You're not gonna hurt Ems.'

Max thought about this, rubbing his stubble.

'Haven't decided yet. I probably will.' He beamed. 'Don't want any loose ends now, do we?'

'Perhaps Martin would like her,' smirked Edwin. 'I've heard she's given him plenty of grief.'

Marie tried to leap at him, her hands outstretched, nails like claws, but was pushed back.

'I've been planning to get rid of you soon, anyway,' Max said to Sharon. 'Nice-looking girl you are to add to my collection. Pity about you, though,' he added, looking at Marie. 'Such a waste of potential having to kill you.'

'Well, don't then,' she spat. 'But I'd like to *kill you*!'

'I expect you would, my dear. Not that I intend to dispose of you straight away. Not when there's money to be made out of you. I think Edwin's got plans to make some really pretty films with you, haven't you, Edwin?'

'I can't wait,' grinned Edwin, leering at Marie. 'She's better than a lot we've had, isn't she?'

'Let me think. The Siberian tigers enjoy a tasty meal. Could make a good wildlife programme, couldn't it, Edwin? Tyger, Tyger, burning bright, in the forests of the night . . .'

'Let's get on with it,' said the Leopard Man. 'You're starting to get poetical and it's always a bad sign.'

'This way, then, children,' Max said, like a showman. 'We'll go back to the castle, then let me take you on a grand tour of the dungeons.'

'Dungeons,' gasped Marie and Slug.

'Dungeons,' I echoed.

'You all thought you'd explored the castle,' Max laughed happily, 'but you didn't know about them, did you? It's such a marvellous castle. I'm so proud of it, and there's always "Moore" of it, little joke.'

The Leopard Man reached out and grabbed Marie. She kicked out, catching him on the shin. He twisted her arm, then pulled her hair painfully.

'Don't try that again,' he warned. 'I've got ways of dealing with badly behaved children.'

'You horrible beast,' she shrieked.

'Leave her alone,' Sharon cried.

'It's no good yelling,' said Max. 'No one's going to help you. So get moving.'

He then walked over to me and grabbed my arm. 'Are you going to be quiet or do I have to hurt you, Brother Gary?' he asked.

For a small man he was very strong. No good struggling.

'Help, help!' Marie yelled. 'Somebody help us!'

'Oh, dear. We'll have to quieten them down. Elastoplast over the mouths, I think. Then into the four-wheel drive and off to the castle. By the special entrance.'

Minder Martin taped up Sharon's mouth and her wrists behind her and then Marie's. I thought her eyes would explode out of her head, she was so angry. Both my sisters were angry, not scared. Ems started to scream.

'Shut that kid up!' Edwin snapped.

Minder Martin went to pick Ems up and she went crazy.

'Naughty Dad-Dad,' she shouted at him, and he dithered just for a minute. Tough. It finished him, for she bit him – on his ear and on his face. Blood spurted like fountains. Howling, he dropped Ems and held his face. He couldn't see.

Slug stopped trembling and flung himself at Edwin. Marie, bound up, did a flying frog jump at Dennis, and Sharon put down her head and butted Max, who let me go.

'Run, Gary, run . . . go for it. Get help! Get help!' Slug yelled.

I moved faster than I ever had in all my life – into the trees, running, running, leaping over tree roots, pushing through brambles, scrambling, flying, as if I'd never spent all my life up till now getting out of races at Sports Day. Bong, bong, bong, bong went my heart, legs churning. But I knew they'd get me. They'd be faster than me once they'd got over the surprise. The trees were thicker now, closer together. I dodged through them and round them – old broad trees thick with green leaves, not nasty old dark needle trees but woodland trees, green, shady, secret.

Breathless now and starting to get a stitch, I had to stop to get my breath. And I could hear the enemy after me with big tramping feet. I leaned for a minute against a huge trunk, older than time and half hollow – could I hide in it? It was dark inside, so thick were the bark and the sprouting leaves. Tripping over a gnarly root, I stretched out my hands to save myself, and they closed round rope – thick, knotted rope – MARSHY! *His* rope, one of his hiding places! Quick as a flash, I was climbing it, up, up, up (I've always hated rope climbing in the gym), up and up and up, higher and higher. When I was as high as I could bear, I stopped and straddled over a fat strong branch, and hauled the rope up after me – it was heavy and tricky but I did it. I lay back panting against the trunk of Super-Tree, my friend. Marshy must often have done this, I thought. The leaves whispered around me. The tree was my saviour. I patted it and felt in my pocket – chewing gum, old and gummy, lovely, bits of anorak on it and all.

Below me as I chewed I could hear the sound of tramping feet and cursing voices. But I was far above all that.

'Tree, I'll pay you back for this, I promise. I'll help Marshy fight for you against the Maxes.'

The noises were fading now. Suddenly I felt tired and trembly. I hoped they were OK. I hoped they didn't get hurt . . . Sharon, Marie, Slug and Ems, oh, and Marshy, too, shut away who knows where.

I'd wait till it was dark and then I'd save them.

Three

When it's dark in a wood it's really dark. I tripped over a tree root and fell flat on my face. Getting up, panic as well as pain hit me in the chest. The night was full of strange noises like a jungly-jungle. What was I doing, playing the hero? I wasn't meant to be a hero. Marie was the hero, not me. She should be doing this, leaping around, getting the police, saving people an' all that, but she'd landed me in it like she always did. Gary will do it. Gary will sort it out. Gary, the mug, the fall guy.

And Gary didn't want to. Shut up, Gary and keep moving on. Moving on.

The moat. If I could get to a phone, I could get help. So I'd got to cross the moat. Suddenly the turreted floodlit castle loomed ahead. The gates had been shut so the people had gone. I hoped I wouldn't run into the photographers. Or maybe I could tell *them*? No, I couldn't handle *that* at all. I crept over the drawbridge into the courtyard and towards the back of this huge dump of a castle. A big wooden door was ahead. I tried it. It was locked.

Now what? The back of the kitchen was near here and I could slip in there, unnoticed, I hoped. I'd just got inside through a small window when I ran into the cook, a large round lady who was always busy cooking and preparing food.

'Git outta here!' she snapped at me. 'Hey, you're the kid Mr Moore told us to keep a lookout for. Stop!'

I rushed round the table as she tried to grab me, sending it flying. Then I dived back through the window head-first and landed in a compost heap. Inside, I could hear the cook shouting for help and moaning that tomorrow's food had been ruined.

I got up, rubbing lumps of compost off me. At least it'd been a soft landing. I bet I looked a right mess now and smelt like a filthy farmyard. No time to worry about that. Voices outside were yelling and torches were sending out beams of light. They'd been alerted. I headed back for the woods near Marshy's den, tripping over roots and branches again. Now to try and get out of here. The voices were further away now.

They'd lost me for the moment. I'd look for help outside the castle, get away from this Enchanted World that'd turned out to be Nightmare Land.

I'd just crept out of the woods and found the road near the entrance leading to the outside world when a car came at me out of the darkness, headlights full-beam, dazzling me. I caught a quick glimpse of Minder Martin behind the wheel of the black limo, looking meaner than a panther, and flung myself out of the way. The car missed me by a matter of inches. Had he seen me? The limo reached the entrance and stopped, blocking it and forcing me back into the estate again. Voices and lights seemed to be everywhere.

I pressed up against the wall surrounding much of the grounds as they got closer. Desperately I scrambled up it, a good six or seven feet high, wobbled on top and landed, guess where, in a muddy ditch on the other side. Now I was covered in mud as well as compost. Still, I was out of that place, over the other side of the wall. Freedom, for now.

I looked back at the drive as I ran and saw the black limo swing round and head out of the gate towards me, a couple of other cars following, so I quickly got off the main road. It was too risky with them looking for me.

I was less panicky now I'd left the castle. If I stayed off the road they shouldn't catch me. But I'd got to find somewhere to call for help and it was bound to be miles to the nearest village. Why did I have to get landed with this? Couldn't I just be a couch potato? Sharon, what have you done to us? Especially me! If I live I'll never forgive you! What do I mean, *if* I live?

The moon came out from behind the clouds and lit up the field. I tried to keep the road in sight as much as possible, 'cos I didn't want to get lost, but I kept in the shadows 'cos I didn't want to be seen. I'd got a stitch and I panted like an engine, but I ran on, spurred by the thought of Marie and all of them trapped in that horrible place.

At the end of another field I could see a cottage in the distance. Maybe I could ask for help there. At last I reached it and banged the knocker hard.

Inside, a dog barked like crazy, then a man cursed and shouted. He opened his bedroom window and glared at me.

'Whatja mean by waking me up and starting

my dog barking?' he shouted angrily. 'Don't you know what time it is?'

'Please, sir, I need your help. I'm in danger,' I stuttered.

'You will be in a minute. I'll send Spike on to you if you don't clear off now!' The window slammed shut.

Sobbing, I ran on, and then joined the road again at a crossroads which told me there was a village (I couldn't read the name) five miles away. I couldn't guess how far I'd gone now. Groaning, I wondered again why Marie couldn't have escaped instead of me. Then I thought, what if Max and Co. were torturing them or something right now? I'd got to keep going till I found help somehow. No choice, Gary, I whimpered to myself.

Car headlights lit up the bend behind me and I shot off the road quickly. If it wasn't for Max's cars I'd try and hitch a lift, but I couldn't risk it. The ground had changed and I was running on bracken and gorse, rough and prickly. And the weather changed too. It began to rain. Mud and compost ran down my face. On I went, breathless, panting, scared, knackered.

A couple of miles further on, I found another house. Second time lucky? I rang the doorbell.

This time a baby started screaming and two cross faces greeted me at the door.

'Why are you ringing our bell at this ungodly hour?' the man demanded.

'Sorry to disturb you, but I think there are some people after me. I need help,' I shouted.

The man stepped outside and took a look around.

'What are you talking about?' he snarled. 'There's nobody out there. Look.'

I did and couldn't see anything.

'Get lost,' said the man. 'We probably won't get any more sleep tonight now you've woken the kid up.' By now the baby was screaming its head off.

'Look at the state of you!' said the woman. 'Shall we let him come in and get cleaned up, do you think? He looks all in.'

'No way. Just push off, will you.'

It looked like I'd be going to the village after all. But I couldn't feel a thing. I'd gone into a sort of overdrive. This was hell and I was there running, dirty, wet and muddy. At last, struggling to the top of a small hill, I could see lights down below.

Faster now I was nearly there, I shot down the

hill and ran down the main road looking for a police building. A blue sign shone out of the darkness. That might be something. Yes, it was. Further up the road.

I stopped short. Oh, no, it can't be! Oh, please! No, no, no, no, no. But yes, it was. By the side of the road was the black limo and Minder Martin was behind the wheel watching.

I ducked down quickly. Had he seen me? He might not have as I'd come from behind the car. How the heck could I get into the police station without him seeing and stopping me? The front door was closed and locked. I ran back up a side street, climbed over a fence and tried to get in the back. But I couldn't open the door and there was no window. I'd *have* to try and get in the front way.

On my stomach, commando style, I wriggled round to the front slowly over the dirt and gravel, who cared? I stretched up a hand and rapped the knocker, keeping an eye on Minder Martin to see if he had heard. There was no reply. I tried again. And again.

The third time he moved in the car. Did he hear me? He was stirring behind the wheel. One more try. If he gets out, I'm off. I wasn't even sure there was anyone there.

I rapped again desperately, louder this time. Come on, if you're there. Come on. Come on. Please. One of the car doors opened. I gave a final rap as loud as I could. If anyone was there they'd just have to hear it.

Then the building suddenly lit up and the car door closed again.

'What is it?' asked a sleepy voice, and a middle-aged man wearily opened the door.

'Please, sir! Can you help me?'

'All right, sonny. Come in.'

I entered the small wooden cabin and looked round. It wasn't exactly Scotland Yard, but among the few pieces of equipment I could see a phone.

'Are you the police around here?' I asked.

'I'm the only policeman here, yes. How can I help you?'

I began to tell him and stopped before I'd finished. He was looking at me as if I'd come down from outer space or escaped from the lunatic asylum or something.

'I don't know what you're on about, sonny boy. Kidnapping, murder, things like that don't happen round here. The only crimes I've had this past year have been a couple of speeding fines and someone stealing a sheep.'

My heart sank. I could see he wasn't the right man to tell. He'd never believe me.

'Look outside. There's a man sitting in a long black car who's after me.'

But the limo had gone.

'Now, son,' he said, patting my head. 'I don't know what you're going on about, but I can see that you're upset about something. There's a washbasin and a bed through here, so why don't you take some rest and clean yourself up and everything will seem different in the morning.'

'Can I phone my mum?' I asked.

'Sure. Go ahead.'

I quickly dialled, but the phone kept ringing at the other end. Mum, Dad, please answer. But Dad wasn't there and Mum was probably looking after Mrs Birkinshaw round her house. Oh, no, no, no. Wasn't there help anywhere? And then . . .

'Can you contact WPC Simmons? She knows me back home.' I gave him her address, but couldn't remember her phone number. What was it? My brain as well as my body was so tired by now. 'She works for the police where I live.'

'Yes, sure, son. You just get washed and rested, OK?'

I went through to the little room and sat

down, rubbed at my face, then stopped, too tired
to wash. I'd tried my best and I was done in.
Would he get through? I could hear the phone
ringing . . .

Much later, I woke up to feel somebody rubbing
my shoulder. There was WPC Katy Simmons
smiling at me.

Four

A convoy of five police cars sped towards the castle. In the back of the first police car sat WPC Simmons with me beside her, and in the front was an Inspector who was running the operation. I'd cleaned myself up as best I could and, being starving hungry, had grabbed a pasty to eat from the village store, so at least I felt human again, and grown-up as well as I sat there telling them about everything that had been happening. They listened, they really listened to me and asked me questions.

When I'd finished the Inspector, a sharp-faced man, said, 'Nothing of what you've told me comes as any great surprise. We have been monitoring the activities of Sir Magnus Moore for some time, but unfortunately have never managed to find any evidence against him. But from what you've been telling me . . . And when we got an anonymous phone call from the castle last night we knew something was blowing up there and we needed to move in.'

'Who d'ya think rang you?'

'We don't know. But it was a female.'

'So you were coming anyway,' I said slowly, gobsmacked. I'd run all that way, about ten miles, getting covered in muck and mud and soaked to the skin, for *nuffink*, YUCK! And I *don't* like running! Who was it phoned, I wondered? All unfair! As ever. It must have shown on my face, for Katy patted my shoulder.

'You're a brave lad, Gary,' she said.

'Do you think they're all right?' I asked, still worried. 'Sharon and Marie and Slug and little Ems? An' Marshy?'

'I'm sure they are, Gary,' said Katy comfortingly. 'You thought he was going to put them in the castle dungeons. It's a huge place, I know.'

'Yeah, but is that all he's done? You can't trust him!'

'Do you think he's flown the coop, sir?' asked the driver sitting beside the Inspector.

What the heck is a coop, I wondered?

'It's possible, but he may well be around somewhere, and if he is, we'll find him.'

'I bet he's been busy getting rid of the evidence,' said the driver.

We arrived at the front entrance to the estate and the Inspector showed his badge to the gateman, who tried to charge us an entrance fee.

'Use your eyes! Police! Let us through,' the Inspector barked.

As the convoy drove through the man spoke into his mobile.

'Bet he's warning Magnus Moore,' said the driver.

'Very likely. But if that's the case it means he's still here,' said the Inspector.

One car stayed behind to block the front entrance and after I told them where the back entrance was, another car was sent there. The remaining cars followed us along to the visitors' car park, now full. I could hear shouts and screams coming from the direction of the theme park. Max's adverts had done the trick. The park was heaving and photographers were everywhere, like old times.

'Do you think we ought to close the place, sir?' asked the driver.

'No, it would cause too much hassle,' replied the Inspector. 'We'll just conduct our operations as discreetly as possible.'

The three police cars pulled up outside the

castle and everyone got out. A couple of pressmen rushed towards us.

'What are you doing here?' one of them asked the Inspector.

'We want to interview Sir Magnus Moore. Do you know where he is?'

'That's just what we were doing when he got a phone call on his mobile and just disappeared into the castle. We tried to follow him, but this big minder stopped us.'

We rushed on with the pressmen in tow.

'You go first and direct us, Gary,' said Katy.

'C'mon. This way.' I was leading them inside when suddenly a thought struck me. 'You'll need the keys for the private room and the dungeon,' I said.

Then in the hall of the castle I saw Nanny Drain Cover guiding a group of visitors around and outlining the history of the place.

'You could ask her. She should know.'

Nanny Drain Cover looked startled as she saw us, and tried to walk away.

'Now, madam,' said the Inspector, 'may I have a word with you?'

'Can you just wait here for a minute?' she asked the group. Reluctantly, she came over to us.

'For the time being, I only have one question for you, madam. Where are the keys to the private room and the dungeon?'

She hesitated.

'I know what's been happening here and if you don't answer I'll have you charged with obstruction.'

'All right,' she muttered. 'I've got a set.' She fumbled in her jacket pockets and produced a large bunch of keys and cards. 'Come on. I'll show you.'

'Thank you. Now lead the way, please.'

Looking terrible, Nanny Drain Cover shot off at speed, leaving the group of visitors bewildered.

'Hey, what's going on? We've paid our entrance fee.'

The private room was open anyway. But all the videos and photographic gear had been removed.

'He's moved all the stuff,' I spluttered.

'That doesn't surprise me. The man's as slippery as an eel,' said the Inspector. 'But he's not going to get away with it this time. Now where?' he demanded.

Following Nanny Drain Cover, we descended those dreaded stairs, down into the depths of the castle, till we arrived outside the huge heavy door, which she unlocked. There we were in the video room where Sharon walloped Beardy. And through the next door.

'Good heavens,' exclaimed the Inspector.

'No, it's the moat,' I explained. 'But where are they? I thought they'd be here! Marie! Sharon! We're coming! Hurry up, won't you?' I shouted. 'They might be dying.'

But they weren't. Behind another door that Nanny Drain Cover unlocked a miserable heap sat on a damp, stone floor, practically in the moat, from the look of it.

'You took your time,' shrieked Marie. 'But I love you, Gary!'

'G-G-Gary – I'll never snore again!' sobbed Slug, trying to hug me. I dodged him, but I couldn't dodge Ems clinging to my legs.

'Dad-Dad,' she screamed and I knew they were all OK.

'This everybody, then?' asked the Inspector. 'No!'

Marie blurted out, 'Max came in here a few minutes ago and took Sharon away, looking real nasty. I tried to stop him, but he had his gun.'

'Oh, no!' cried Katy.

'Come on,' shouted the Inspector as we ran up the stairs, Ems on Katy's back.

'Do you think he'll take revenge on her or somethin'?' I asked.

'I hope not. But he might use her as a hostage,' she warned.

The Inspector busily briefed his team.

'We're going to search this castle and estate from top to bottom for this man,' he said, showing a picture of Max. 'He may be accompanied by a young lady, his wife, so play it carefully. No heroics. I don't want her life endangered. Now let's get going!'

'Are you going to fill us in on what's going on?' asked the pressmen, streaming through the castle and grounds.

'No comment,' said the Inspector.

Five

The Inspector and his team started to go over the castle like Mum searching for nits. We shoved Ems in a buggy and followed just behind because he kept trying to send us back.

Minder Martin took a lot of persuading to go quietly and Leopard Man was only just stopped sneaking out through a side gate. But Max? Nowhere!

'The helicopter,' shouted Marie. 'Come on!' We ran ahead while they followed. When we all reached the barn we found the door open and a man dressed in overalls measuring up the damage. When he saw us he tried to close the door, but the Inspector stopped him.

'I'm looking in there,' he said, charging in.

There he was, Max, standing near the back of the barn behind Sharon, still in her dirty shirt, looking tired and fed up, not a heavenly beauty any more, just ole Sharon.

'Would you come with us, please, Sir Magnus?

There's a number of questions we'd like you to answer. And you can let the girl go.'

Max gripped Sharon and held her closer to him. 'I'll answer them here, if that's all right. You've got no grounds to arrest me.'

'I arrest you on the charge of torturing children to make movies.'

'What are you talking about? I make costume and historical dramas.'

'And kidnapping and imprisoning people in dungeons.'

'That was only for a dare. A competition to see who could stay there the longest. Had enough already, have they?'

'And murdering and feeding people to the lions and tigers. Killing your wives and making waxworks of them.'

'Poppycock. You've got no proof of any of this and you know it.'

Max seemed completely cool. Sharon didn't say anything, just looked at us. Maybe she had a gun in her back. You couldn't see his right hand, which was behind her.

'Now, since I've answered these ridiculous allegations, may I go about my business and take my wife on a helicopter ride which I promised her before?' Max paused and looked at me suspiciously, '*Someone* broke in here and smashed the windscreen, among other things.' He glared at us.

'You gonna drop her out of it or somethin'?' I hissed.

'By the way, your accomplices are now in custody ready to give evidence about the activities taking place here,' said the Inspector.

Max's manner changed and he stepped forward, holding a gun at Sharon's back.

'Right then, the charade's over now,' he snapped. 'You got it ready yet?' he shouted at the mechanic.

'Not really. There's bin some real damage done to it,' he replied.

'Then we'll go by car.' Max pointed at the Land Rover parked on the grass. 'You,' he said, pointing the gun at WPC Simmons, 'can drive. And I'll bring *him* along too. I've got a score to settle with him!'

He glinted at me. Then, holding the gun in Sharon's back, he came out into the open, edged his way past us over to the car and opened the door. The police stood helpless, unable to act. He made me get in the front with Katy and he got in the back with Sharon, sitting behind Katy in the driver's seat.

'Get rid of those cars blocking the entrances,' he told the Inspector through the open window. 'Let's get cracking, then,' he said to Katy.

'You won't get away with this, you know,' she said as she started up the Land Rover. In the mirror I could see the Inspector speaking urgently into his radio.

'Shut up! No talking unless I say so. And no tricks, right!' Max said, gun trained on Sharon. 'Then you lot might get out of this alive . . .' He paused. 'If you're lucky. But, then again, I might kill you anyway. You've caused me a lot of bother!'

We bumped along over the rough ground and joined the main road running through the estate.

'We'll go the back way,' said Max. 'Less busy.'

I felt like crying, scared of wetting myself. My mum often says, 'Out of the frying pan into the fire.' That was us. I thought we'd be all right when I got the police, but now we were really in trouble 'cos I knew Max intended to kill us. Why not? Killing people didn't bother him. He'd done it before.

Though the estate was crowded there was hardly a soul on this stretch of road leading to the back entrance. Max had chosen his escape route well. It was bumpy 'cos we were driving along the bit of road the construction gang had been working on, but hadn't finished yet. It led past the theme park, which suddenly came into view, and we could hear the happy shrieks and shouts and yells of people whizzing and zooming on the rides. But the biggest one of all, standing apart from the rest, Armageddon, was standing still, men working on it. They hadn't managed to get it running on time after all.

Then we turned a corner to find Joe the lion standing there, ragged looking as ever, right in the middle of the road.

'It's that awful lion!' cried Sharon. 'Watch out!'

'Who let that blasted animal out?' snarled Max. 'That blockhead Dennis!'

Katy swerved to avoid him, the car skidded across the road and shot into a ditch, two wheels overhanging the edge. The door on Max's side flew open and in a flash Joe was there, roaring and snarling for once. He sank his one good tooth into Max's leg. This was our chance . . .

'C'mon,' I yelled, and we jumped out of our seats and through the car door to safety, I hoped, Katy following just behind us as we fled up the road.

'I don't think that lion likes Max somehow,' I

said, listening to screams even louder than those of the crowd.

Then we heard a shot and looking round, I saw that Max was out of the car, hobbling down the road clutching his gnawed leg.

Katy was yelling into her radio. 'Suspect on foot now heading for theme park. Hostages safe now. All units can go!'

A police car which had been following us slowly suddenly overtook and drove on in pursuit, sirens screaming.

Now we were safe I wanted to see what was gonna happen. So did Marie, who had caught us up, red-faced and panting. She never liked to miss out on anything. She'd left Slug to look after Ems, she said. We ran after the police car and found it further up the road, empty, for the police were now chasing Max on foot.

'There he is,' Sharon cried.

We could see him now, on the wrong side of the fence from the theme park, heading for a gate further along.

'Do you think he may try and take another prisoner?' shouted Marie.

In the nearby theme park the happy visitors screamed and shouted. They didn't know what was going on all around them.

'He won't get much chance,' I said. 'They're closin' in on him now.'

From all angles they came, the police converging on the park. Max was half running, half dragging his injured leg with one hand, the gun in the other. A rat caught in a trap. He went through the gate by the Amageddon ride. The police surrounded him there. Nowhere else to escape. He headed over to a worker in control of the ride, waving his gun.

'Give up, Sir Magnus,' roared the Inspector through a megaphone over the noise of the crowd. 'You can't get away.'

'Get it started,' snarled Max to the worker.

'But, sir, it's not ready. There are still some technical problems . . .'

'DO IT!'

Max hauled himself into one of the cars as the machinery shuddered into motion. With the police, we watched as the huge ride started with its one passenger. It zoomed into the air and travelled right round the outside of the park in a series of corkscrew turns, loops, twists, getting faster and faster and faster until it reached a finale, the death-defying drop down to earth through grey whirling mist into a black tunnel. It shot downwards like a missile, and we watched to see it reappear at the other end as it was supposed to. But it didn't. Instead there was a huge crash, followed by a bang, then an explosion which rocked the whole theme park to its foundations.

Crowds were heading for the accident zone in droves, photographers by the dozen. So were we, until stopped by Katy.

'You don't want to see him. He'll be smashed to bits.'

'I told him it wasn't ready,' the man bawled over the now silent crowd.

The Inspector called out through his megaphone. 'Can you people move on, please? There's nothing to see now.'

The police started to cordon off the area and the crowd drifted back to the other rides.

Six

A small, dirty figure was running towards us. As he drew near you could see he'd got a black eye and a battered face. He didn't look up to much, but Sharon gave a great screech and shot forward.

'Oh, Marshy, Marshy! I thought . . .'

But what she thought got lost in all the hugging and kissing. Not that Sharon's thoughts were ever up to much anyway. But I remembered something I'd wanted to tell him.

'Marshy,' I yelled as they went away wrapped tight round each other. 'I'll help you save those trees.'

But he didn't answer. He didn't even seem to be listening.

'Hi, Gary! I hear you're a hero.' Purdey was beaming at me. 'I shall give you a kiss.'

I tried to stop going red. I mean, in my book, FEMALES IS RUBBISH – Sharon and

Marie and Ems are enough to put you off them for life. But Purdey – well, Purdey's different.

After she'd kissed me (more than once) and given me some special chocolate she'd pinched as she'd run past a stall, I started to tell her all about Max's evil ways.

'I know . . .' she said. 'You see, I'm Purdey Sims.'

'You mean, Polly was your sister? Oh, I'm so sorry.'

'Yeah. That's why I came here as a maid. To find out what had happened to her. And I think, Gary, he killed her . . .'

She turned away. I patted her, 'cos she was crying.

'Can I come and live with you? It'd be great to get away from Sharon and Marie and Ems. They're all horrible in their different ways, you see. And then you wouldn't miss Polly if you'd got me.'

She'd stopped crying and was laughing now.

'I'll see.'

'And what's the matter with you, Marie? You're crying, too.'

'Joe's dead,' Marie sniffed. 'He wasn't much of a lion, but he didn't have to die.'

'He died saving us,' I said.

'I know. But I think saving you was a waste of a good lion!'

There was more weeping and wailing as we were joined by Mum and Dad, who'd arrived to take us home. Ems hit Dad hard with Blah on the nose and he howled for a different reason. Slug wept more than anyone else as usual.

This was all a bit much and I wanted to leave straightaway. I couldn't wait to get back to ordinary life again. But Marie insisted, much to Dad's annoyance, on burying Joe before we went. He had to dig the grave.

Marie made a little cross with a card on it, 'For Joe. King of the Lions', which was over the top, I thought.

Purdey and Katy promised to visit us.

When I got back home I slept and slept. For ever, it seemed.

'Was this holiday exciting enough for you?' I asked Marie later.

'You bet. But I don't mind being bored for a bit. Not for long, though.'

'Max went out with a bang, didn't he? I bet you're glad you didn't go on that ride now!'

'I'd still like to sometime, when it's working proper.'

'As long as you don't expect me to. I've gone off them.'

'Gary, don't tell Mum everything about our holiday. She'll never let us go away on our own again and it was pretty excitin' really.'

I gazed at her, speechless, After this I never felt like going on holiday again ever. Especially to castles or theme parks. I'd seen enough of them to last a lifetime.

The historic Moore Grave estate, castle and theme park is to be sold off and some of the proceeds divided between the families of Sir Magnus Moore's victims. No one has come to take it over at present because it has a reputation for being haunted owing to the number of bodies believed buried there. The National Trust has expressed an interest.

The newest, biggest theme park of all time is being constructed on a distant island in the South Pacific. Organizing this project is Mr Regan Roomer, a small man with red curls, ginger designer stubble and horn-rimmed spectacles. He is accompanied by a lovely young girl with cropped black hair.

*

Everyone thought we'd be millionaires now, but we didn't get any money. Sharon's not interested in money anyway, as she and Marshy are too busy saving the planet. But Marie emptied out her savings and we splashed out on a midnight feast with Slug and Ems. It was much better than Max's ole parties.